Autumn Skies over Ruby Falls

HOLLY MARTIN

CHAPTER ONE

Clover Philips made her way back to the hotel reception. She was hot and sweaty after teaching her Friday Irish dancing class for the last hour but she had some emails she needed to send before she could go and have a shower. She caught sight of herself in one of the gold mirrors that hung in the corridors – her blonde hair was a tangled bush; her face was shiny and red and she had the biggest smile on her face.

Teaching dance had always been a dream of hers but not something she'd ever really had the opportunity to do before, despite all her qualifications and experience in it. The closest she'd got was teaching yoga, Pilates and other fitness classes in a big gym in London, but it was always dance she was most interested in.

Now that she was a partner in her family hotel, her dreams had come true. Six months before, at her dad's will reading, it had become apparent that her dad had sold part of the hotel before he'd died to Noah Campbell, a hotel developer. And although she and her sisters, Aria and Skye, had initially been horrified at the thought of losing part of their family home,

Noah had turned out to be the best thing to happen to it. The hotel had been in a bad state of repair before he'd come. He'd completely redecorated every room and area of the hotel and brought with him a huge wealth of experience in terms of making the hotel better and getting more customers through the door.

With the new renovations in the Sapphire Bay Hotel had come a new dance studio and now Clover taught Irish dancing, jive, tap, ballet, ballroom and many other styles of dance to the villagers who lived on Jewel Island and the hotel guests. She couldn't be happier.

Her dad had always wanted her to follow her dreams and open up her own dance studio. He would have been delighted to see her doing just that in his hotel. Despite the sad fact that he had died over eighteen months before, she still considered it his hotel, although it was now her and her sisters' responsibility to ensure it flourished and to make him proud.

She walked back into her office and instinctively checked her mobile phone. She noticed she had a WhatsApp message and her heart leapt. She quickly opened it and saw it was a reply from Angel, following on from their conversation earlier about his forthcoming stay.

See you soon x

She couldn't help the huge smile from spreading across her face. This next week before he arrived was going to drag by. She'd become really good friends with Angel Mazzeo over the last few months, since he'd arrived at the hotel as Noah Campbell's assistant. It was because of Noah that the hotel had changed beyond all recognition and that it was now full almost every weekend and at least three-quarters full during the week. But it was because of Angel that Clover's heart, which had been firmly closed to any hint of a relationship for the last three years, had started opening again.

Nothing had happened between them and she wasn't sure if anything ever would, or whether it was too late for that now. He had asked her out to dinner several months before, but she'd told him she wasn't ready for a relationship yet. Surprisingly, as he struck her as the kind of man who would have a different girlfriend every week, he'd told her he was quite happy to wait. Since then they'd fallen well and truly into the friendzone. She was quite content there; it was safe and Angel was lovely. He travelled a lot with his job and sometimes whole months would go by without her seeing him but they kept in touch, talking or messaging several times a day. When he came home next week, he'd be back for several months at least. Maybe, just maybe, she might be able to move their relationship forward a little.

The hotel was holding a Halloween ball on Sunday, which was just nine days away. There was going to be a three-course meal, dancing, and the whole thing was to be in fancy dress. This was Clover's baby and had taken a lot of organising but she was also really looking forward to it. She wanted to prove that the hotel was capable of holding big events like this in the hope she could get more party and wedding bookings in the future. But mostly she was looking forward to it because she had kind of hoped that Angel might want to come with her, if she was brave enough to ask him. The thought of that filled her with excitement and fear in equal measure and she wasn't sure which emotion would win.

Still, she had a week to come up with a plan and decide what she was going to do and maybe, with a little or a lot of help from her sisters, Skye and Aria, she could finally put the past behind her and move on once and for all.

She looked out the window at the beautiful maple tree that was filled with leaves of scarlet, gold and amber. The leaves danced in the autumn breeze and glowed under the rays of the setting sun. Change was definitely in the air, maybe in more ways than one.

She clicked open her email account and scanned through to see what replies she'd had. In between all her dance classes, she was attempting to set the hotel up as a wedding and events venue. That had always been her mum and dad's dream – well, her mum's dream mainly, but after her mum died when Clover was only ten, that dream had been put on hold. Skye and Aria thought the wedding venue idea was a great one but they weren't as passionate about it as she was. One of Clover's fondest memories as a child was walking around the gardens with her mum, listening to her explain how the weddings would be set up in the gardens, overlooking Sapphire Bay. The flower arches, the white chairs. People mingling around in the sunshine, drinking champagne. Clover could picture it all so vividly and she wanted that for the hotel so much.

There was a wedding booked for Christmas, the first in the hotel, but it was only going to be a small affair and if they were really going to showcase what the hotel could offer they were going to have to fake it. A photographer had been booked for Sunday, they had various models coming, they were going to dress the restaurant and various parts of the hotel and then they were going to fake a wedding and put all the resulting photos on the hotel website.

She sent a quick reply to the agent for the models confirming that a vegetarian lunch for two of the models would be available. She opened up another email to see the list of photos the photographer was going to take. She had been very specific that it was important to take some shots outside to capture the magnificent views of Sapphire Bay and the rest of Jewel Island. The hotel was in a beautiful location off the Cornish coast and she wanted to showcase it. She'd even thought about capturing some photos by the waterfall near her cottage in the hotel grounds – it could look particularly dramatic.

She was just writing out a quick email to the photographer to suggest that when she heard voices outside in the reception area.

'I'm sorry but we're fully booked,' Xena, one of the hotel receptionists, said.

'There has to be something, I'd only need a single bed,' said a voice her heart recognised a few seconds before her head did. 'Or even a Z-bed set up in the corner somewhere would be fine.'

Clover scrabbled out of her seat so fast she knocked it over and ran to the door. There was Angel Mazzeo leaning over the reception desk wearing one of his silly t-shirts which showed off the muscles in his arms perfectly. This t-shirt had a giraffe wearing a tie standing proudly on it. He'd had a haircut since the last time she'd seen him. It was much shorter at the sides but messier and spikier at the top as if no effort had gone into styling it at all. Her heart filled at the sight of him.

He glanced over at her and his whole face lit up in a big smile. She found herself running forward and he opened his arms and enveloped her in a big hug.

'Angel Mazzeo. What are you doing here?' Clover said, holding him tight.

'I said I'd see you soon,' Angel said.

'I thought you meant next week, not in a few hours.'

She looked up at him. He'd caught the sun after being in Dubai for the last month or so. It made his blue eyes even more startling.

He smiled. 'I wanted to surprise you.'

'Well you did that. The best kind of surprise.'

'Although it kind of backfired a bit. There's no room at the inn.'

'No, it's half term, school holidays. Plus there's the Halloween festival – so many people have turned up for that and we're completely full.'

'We'll have a room next weekend, one of the suites will be available Saturday and Sunday night,' Tilly, the other receptionist, said helpfully.

Angel smiled gratefully at her.

'Look, I've been travelling for around thirty hours. I just need somewhere to sleep for a few hours and then I can go back to the mainland and find a hotel there.'

'Well, Clover has a spare room in her cottage,' Tilly said, giving Clover a wink. 'I'm sure she wouldn't mind you crashing there.'

Clover felt her mouth fall open at the blatant matchmaking. Were her feelings for Angel that obvious? Although it wouldn't be the first time that the islanders or even the regular hotel guests had tried to interfere. They'd all seen how close she and Angel had become over the last few months and were quite happy to drop little hints here and there. It had never been as obvious as Tilly's attempt though. Clover almost wanted to laugh except it had now got just a little bit awkward. Angel was watching her carefully. She could hardly turn him down now, make up some lame excuse that he would see straight through. And he was her friend, she could help him out. It wasn't odd for him to sleep in her spare room, it made perfect sense, so why was she making it weird?

She cleared her throat. 'Of course you can sleep with me.'

Angel's eyebrows shot up into his hair, Tilly giggled, Xena gasped, and it almost seemed like the entire reception area had gone silent with that declaration.

'Well, I'd like that very much,' Angel said, a smirk of amusement playing on his lips.

Clover laughed, breaking the tension. 'I meant stay with me. In my spare bedroom, not in my bed, you pervert.'

'Well, I'd like that slightly less, but I'd honestly be happy with any bed right now, and your lovely company will be an added bonus.'

She smiled. This was absolutely fine. They were two friends who could just chat and hang out and it wouldn't be weird or romantic at all.

'Aww, see, this has worked out perfectly,' Tilly said. 'You can sit in front of that gorgeous log fire, maybe share a glass or two of wine as you look out over the beautiful falls. It almost sounds... romantic.'

Clover flashed her a look but Tilly clearly didn't care. One of the hazards of having someone you'd known your entire life working at the hotel was that they thought they had carte blanche to interfere as much as they liked. Well, Tilly clearly did. Clover had once asked Tilly why she was working there after her years spent in a high-paid advertising job. Tilly had simply answered, for the gossip. Clearly, today she was in her element.

Clover turned her attention back to Angel. 'I'm pretty much done here for the day. Let me just close down my laptop and I'll be with you.'

'No rush,' Angel said.

She went back to her office, quickly righting her chair before Angel saw it. She closed her computer down as he appeared in the doorway. She tried not to be frantic with her movements – she didn't need him to know how excited she was to see him, although perhaps that ship had already sailed after the way she had thrown herself at him as soon as he walked through the door. She tidied a few things away, very aware he was watching her. She grabbed her phone and put it back in her bag, pulled on her coat and joined him.

'I normally walk to my house as it's only about ten or fifteen minutes away but we'll take the golf buggy as you've got your suitcase,' Clover said.

'I don't normally mind a walk, but today I'll take you up on that buggy. I'm knackered.'

She waved goodbye to Xena and Tilly who gave her a big thumbs up and an eyebrow wiggle behind Angel's back as they walked out. Clover let out a little sigh to herself. By the end of the day the whole of Jewel Island would know that Angel was staying at Clover's. They'd assume that they'd be at it like rabbits, which rather annoyingly couldn't be further from the truth.

Angel threw his suitcase in the back of the golf buggy as Clover got behind the wheel. He sat next to her and she moved off towards her cottage at Ruby Falls. The trees above them were a canopy of copper and gold and she tried to focus on that and not on the man sitting beside her. A cool wind blew off the sea and she thought about lighting a fire when she got into her home, except that it now had romantic connotations attached to it thanks to Tilly.

She glanced at Angel who was enjoying the view, with seemingly no idea of the turmoil she was putting herself through. Her heart was thundering nervously and she had no idea why. She'd known him for around six months, he was her friend and he was just so utterly lovely. But they both knew there was an underlying attraction between them, their chemistry had been sparking in the air every time they were together. This was the first time he would be in her space and it wasn't just that he'd be sleeping under the same roof, he'd also be sharing her bathroom, albeit not at the same time. God, this was suddenly feeling like a really bad idea.

But why? She'd been gearing up to ask him out for weeks or months and, though she'd never been brave enough to change that dynamic between them and start a relationship, even if it was casual, she couldn't deny there was a huge part of her that wanted that, that wanted to be brave and have a normal, fun relationship again. Maybe this was the chance she'd been looking for.

'I like your hair by the way,' Angel said.

Clover blushed, remembering it was a tangled bush; she almost always had it up.

'My hair tie broke at the start of my dancing lesson. It gets a little out of control if there's nothing there to tame it.'

He reached out and took a blonde curl in his fingers. 'I like it. It looks like you've just got out of bed after a night of passion.'

Clover kept her eyes on the road as they made their way up the hill. Passion had been missing from her life for a long time. The feel of his hand in her hair was wonderful. She looked over at him, and his eyes were filled with mischief, as if he was thinking about spending a night of passion with her. God, she wanted that with him so much but her fears were holding her back.

They drove past Ruby Falls, the setting sun glinting off the water as it tumbled down the rocks into the deep plunge pool below.

She pulled up outside Ruby Cottage and hopped down from the golf buggy. She loved her little home painted the colour of rosé wine. It had views over the falls from the front and views of Sapphire Bay and Pearl Beach from behind. It was secluded here, quiet. And then there were the animals: three horses, a cow and sometimes a donkey which she had somehow adopted over the last year or so. Two of the horses were currently leaning over the fence watching her hopefully in case she'd sneaked any carrots or apples from the hotel for them.

She stroked the nose of Bob, a gorgeous black and white piebald. He whickered softly. Angel came up by her side and stroked Freya's neck.

'What a beautiful palomino,' Angel said, softly. Freya nodded her head as if to agree. 'Are they yours?'

'Sort of. They belong to the farm next door, but the farmer asked me to look after them while he went on holiday and then never came back. So yes, they're my responsibility now.'

Clover stepped away and let herself into her cottage. It was a small place inside and it suddenly felt all the smaller when Angel moved inside with her and closed the door behind him. Her heart fluttered as he stared at her, excitement over having him here being quashed with the fear of what might happen between them.

Orion, her beautiful calico cat and the latest addition to her menagerie, strolled over to investigate the new arrival, winding his way around Angel's legs and purring loudly. Angel bent down to scratch behind Orion's ears.

'That's Orion and he flirts with everything that moves,' Clover said.

'Nothing wrong with that, eh Orion?' Angel said.

Clover smiled. Angel was definitely the sort of man that enjoyed flirting with women. There was probably a trail of broken hearts wherever he had been. That should have been enough to make her wary about getting involved with him, but funnily enough it wasn't. She knew if anything was to ever happen between them, it wouldn't be serious. Angel just wasn't the settling-down and happy-ever-after type and she was OK with that.

'I'll show you your room,' Clover said. She went up the stairs and Angel followed her, carrying his suitcase with him. 'I actually put fresh sheets on the spare bed a few days ago as Jesse is here and Skye thought it might be a good idea if they maintained some distance rather than their weird friends-with-benefits arrangement.'

Her twin sister Skye had a complicated relationship with her ex-husband. Complicated in that they were both still crazy in love with each other but neither wanted to admit they had feelings for each other.

Angel let out a bark of a laugh. 'Knowing Skye and Jesse, that sleeping arrangement probably lasted five seconds after Jesse arrived.'

'Yes, Jesse didn't even set foot in here, so the bed is clean, I promise.'

'The way I'm feeling right now, I wouldn't even care if it wasn't.'

They walked into the bedroom and she felt the tension crackle in the air between them as they both stared at the bed.

Angel cleared his throat. 'Thanks for this, I really appreciate it. And as a thank you, why don't I cook dinner for us tonight? After I've slept for a few hours, that is.'

'You're assuming I have food in for you to cook. I normally eat at the hotel with my sisters.'

'Well, why don't I order us some pizza from the Italian in the village. I, um... have something I'd like to ask you.'

'What's that?'

He smiled. 'It's probably better if I ask you over pizza and wine.'

Clover stared at him, that feeling of panic rising in her. What did he want to say? Was he going to ask her out? Was she ready for that? 'I'm actually really looking forward to hearing all about your trip to Dubai.'

God, why was she back-pedalling away from him? She hated her indecisiveness and her fears. She was tired of being scared. Why couldn't she just be normal again? But Marcus, her ex, had damaged her and she didn't know if she'd ever feel normal about dating ever again.

He frowned slightly at the spanner she'd just thrown in the works. 'Well, we can certainly talk about that too.'

She knew she'd have to come up with lots of questions about Dubai now, keep him talking about that so he'd have no time to bring up anything else.

'I'll leave you to sleep,' Clover said, scooting out the door and closing it behind her.

She went back downstairs and scooped up Orion, plopping him over her shoulder and stroking along his silky back.

The floor creaked above her as Angel got into bed.

'Orion, what am I going to do?'

Orion purred into her shoulder, giving her no help at all beyond his physical comfort.

She grabbed her phone and sat down, with Orion sprawled across her lap. She opened up her WhatsApp group with her sisters and quickly wrote a message.

Help! Angel has arrived and because there was no room at the hotel, he's now staying at my house – in my spare room before you get any weird ideas. And now I'm freaking out because there's all this chemistry sparking in the air between us. He's gone to sleep now and we're having pizzas later from Bella's and he says he wants to talk to me over dinner tonight. I'm not ready.

She pressed send, feeling like a complete idiot and hating Marcus, her ex-boyfriend, just that little bit more right then because he had messed her up spectacularly.

Her identical twin, Skye, was the first to reply.

I'm just finishing up at the café. Me and Jesse will be there in about an hour.

Oh no, she didn't want them there to babysit her, she just wanted some words of advice and moral support.

Clover had started writing out a message to say that it

wasn't necessary when another message from Skye came through.

I'll bring ice cream.

That was Skye's cure for everything. Owning her own dessert café in the grounds of the hotel, Skye was the pudding and ice cream queen. Clover was quite sure that the desserts contained magical ingredients because she always felt better after eating them. She could really do with some ice cream round about now.

A message from Aria, her older sister, popped through.

We'll be there too. Noah has a ton of questions for Angel about what went on in Dubai. We'll bring the pizzas.

Well this had suddenly escalated. It would look like she was bringing in reinforcements. Clover felt bad for Angel; after thirty hours of travelling, the last thing he needed was the Spanish Inquisition or for there to be lots of people here when he just wanted to chill out and relax.

Still, the more people there the better and maybe she could avoid any awkward conversations with Angel for a little while longer.

CHAPTER TWO

Skye and Aria arrived at the same time with Jesse and Noah in tow, they had boxes of pizzas and snacks with them. Clover wondered if they had been talking about her situation on the way up to the cottage and coming up with a plan of attack. Her sisters, although completely supportive of her issues, were perhaps even more keen to see her and Angel get together than Clover was.

'Where is he?' Noah asked as they walked into her lounge, after they'd greeted each other.

'He's asleep, he's been up for over thirty hours. He'll probably be up soon, he said he just wanted a few hours' rest,' Clover said.

'I'm sorry that there's no room for him in the hotel,' Aria said. 'If I'd known he was coming, I would have booked one of the rooms for him. Even the suites are filled this week.'

'It's OK,' Clover said. 'I don't mind having him here.'

'We have a spare room in our apartment,' Aria said, looking at Noah. 'He could sleep in there.'

Noah's eyes widened at the prospect of having his assistant

in the bedroom next door to him and Aria. By all accounts, their night-time activities were very noisy. Poor Angel didn't need to hear that.

'My spare room doesn't even have a bed right now but Jesse could sleep here with Angel and me and you could share a bed in my cottage,' Skye said.

Jesse didn't look too happy with that suggestion either.

'Honestly, it's fine,' Clover said.

'I just don't want you to feel uncomfortable in your own home,' Skye said and Clover smiled with love for her twin.

'I'm not uncomfortable about having him here, I'm just… not looking forward to talking to him about what I think he wants to talk to me about.'

Clover sighed. She sounded like a teenager about to go out on her first-ever date.

Aria turned to Jesse and Noah, ushering them into the kitchen. 'Why don't you go and warm up the pizzas and get the drinks and snacks ready.'

As soon as they were gone, Clover flopped down on the sofa and Skye and Aria joined her.

'What's wrong with me? Angel is sweet and kind—'

'And gorgeous,' Skye said.

'Hey!' Jesse said, from the kitchen.

Skye giggled.

'That too,' Clover said. 'Why can't I take that step with him?'

'Because Marcus was complete and utter scum and what he did to you was disgusting. If that had happened to me, I don't think I'd ever get over it,' Aria said.

'Thanks,' Clover said, sadly. This wasn't exactly filling her with hope.

'But you have to, because Marcus would be delighted if he

saw you now, unable to move on because of him. And you can't give him that,' Skye said.

Anger bubbled up inside of her. Skye was right. She couldn't let Marcus win. 'You're right. I know you are. But how do I move forward? It's been so long since I've been in a relationship, I'm not even sure how to have one, or which bits go where.'

Skye laughed. 'Trust me, that part is like riding a bike, you never forget.'

Aria took Clover's hand. 'You move forward by, firstly, choosing someone who is lovely, sweet, patient and kind, someone you trust.'

'I do trust Angel and he is all of those things.'

'And then, you tell him, all of it, so he knows what you are dealing with and can help you through it.'

Clover groaned. 'I'm pretty sure Angel is the kind of man who has had more girlfriends than hot dinners. I'm not sure if he is signing up for that level of baggage from me. I know he likes me, but he probably thinks we'd get together, have fun, have some great sex and that would be it. And there's a huge part of me that wants that too. I'm not looking for something serious. There's no way I'm ready for that. I just want to have a normal, fun relationship with someone lovely so I can finally move on from Marcus once and for all. We've not even kissed yet, I don't want to scare Angel off with all my issues.'

Noah appeared in the doorway. 'I think Angel is well aware that this is something more than just a casual one-night stand for you. He knows you're holding back and you're scared, but he doesn't know why. And despite any baggage you might have, Angel still clearly wants to pursue something with you. You're right that he has had his fair share of girlfriends since I've known him, but that doesn't mean he's not capable of something a bit more serious. I think you should give him more credit. He's a really great bloke, you know that.'

Clover nodded. That part was true at least. Angel was one of the loveliest men she had ever met.

Noah came in and placed the pizzas on the coffee table in the lounge and Jesse followed him.

'I don't know Angel as well as all of you,' Jesse said in his soft Canadian accent. 'But he doesn't strike me as the sort of man who would do a runner at the first sign of drama. I think you should tell him and if he doesn't want to stick around then he wasn't the right man for you anyway.'

Skye smiled proudly at her ex-husband. 'Couldn't have said it better myself.'

Clover sighed but she knew they were right. She couldn't start a relationship with Angel, no matter how casual, unless he knew the truth. Now she just had to pluck up the courage to tell him.

Angel stood at the top of the stairs, feeling bad that he'd heard Clover's conversation with her sisters. The scent of delicious pizza and the voices of Skye, Aria, Jesse and Noah had woken him up. He should have known they would be there. He'd seen the panic in Clover's eyes when he'd said he wanted to talk to her. They had grown so close over the last few months and he'd wanted to ask if she was ready to start dating again. She must have guessed what he wanted to say. It was safe to say that conversation wasn't going to happen tonight. He wouldn't be at all surprised if Clover had asked her sisters to come round purely so she wouldn't have to talk to him.

He would just have to put a pin in that conversation for now. He didn't want her feeling awkward or tense in her own home. He would give her time to relax with having him back again and maybe in a few days he would be able to bring it up with her.

He had no idea what he was up against here. He knew she had feelings for him. There was a hell of a lot more than just friendship between them. There was this spark there every time they were together. But she was wary of getting involved with someone again and he had no idea why, other than he now knew her ex-boyfriend had clearly done something horrible.

He went into the bathroom and took a quick shower, letting the hot water wash away any travel fatigue, at least for the next few hours.

Clover didn't want anything serious, she wanted something fun to help her get over her ex. He could do that. He'd spent almost his entire life having only casual relationships with women. He had no intention of settling down yet, there was too much world to see, too much he didn't want to miss out on. So why did he feel a tiny bit disappointed with that? No, actually, he was quite happy to have some fun with Clover, if she could trust him enough to take that step.

He got dressed and went downstairs. Clover immediately leapt up, guilt written all over her face.

'Let me get you some pizza,' she said, plating up a couple of slices. 'Everyone was so keen to see you again, I hope you don't mind they all came over.'

Angel smiled and took the pizza, sitting down to eat it. He looked around the room at his supposed welcome party. Noah, his boss, would certainly be keen to discuss the sale of one of his hotels in Dubai and how that had gone, although Angel was pretty sure Noah would have been happy to wait until the next day to talk through that with him properly. Noah's girlfriend, Aria, the manager of the Sapphire Bay

Hotel, was lovely and they'd always got on well but he wouldn't expect her to rush round to see him the second he'd stepped off the plane. Skye, Clover's identical twin, was so different to Clover; she was bold where Clover was quiet. She was also fiercely protective of her sister and Skye had already warned him to be careful with Clover, many months ago. And although Skye had not said the words, the threat had been very clear. *You hurt her and I'll hurt you.* He liked Skye, but he couldn't say he had really become good friends with her. And Jesse he'd only met once before when he'd come over to help Skye get her ice cream café ready in the spring. He seemed like a decent enough bloke and clearly adored Skye but, again, he and Angel weren't exactly friends.

This wasn't a welcome party, they were here to chaperone Clover.

He took a bite of his pizza and noticed there was an air of wariness in the room.

Orion, the cat that had welcomed him earlier, was far more forthcoming, curling himself around Angel's legs. Angel stroked under his chin.

Noah leaned forward. 'It's good to have you back. So the sale all went well in the end?'

'Yes, very smoothly. I mean, your solicitors handled all that side of things, but the transition with all the staff went well. I think they felt ready for a change. Many of them are excited to be working with Starburst Heights Hotels and I think the promise of increased pay helped to smooth over any ruffled feathers.'

'I'm glad you were there, you have a way of keeping everyone calm.'

'I'm happy to help. Also it's Dubai, one of the most beautiful places in the world. It wasn't exactly a hardship.'

Angel knew that Noah felt a bit guilty about leaving Angel

to handle everything for him. Noah had spent years buying, developing and selling hotels around the world and they had always been a team in every aspect of that process. But since Noah had got together with Aria, he'd wanted to stay here on Jewel Island as much as possible and Angel didn't blame him. But Noah also knew that Angel liked to travel, to see the world. Angel had itchy feet, this urge to see it all, and working with Noah in different hotels in various countries allowed him to scratch that itch. It suited them both for Angel to continue doing these things on Noah's behalf.

'What's Dubai like?' Clover asked.

'It's an incredible place, it's out of this world. There's a building called the Dubai Frame which is basically just a huge gold photo frame that's around a hundred and fifty metres high. You can go up to the top and there is a glass floor that you can walk on hundreds of feet in the air.'

'That sounds terrifying,' Clover said.

He watched her carefully. 'I think sometimes it's good to do something that scares us, push ourselves out of our comfort zone just a little bit, be brave. Most of the time, you know you aren't going to fall.'

Clover stared at him. It was quite obvious he wasn't really talking about the glass walkway. He wouldn't push it tonight but he wanted her to know that if she took that chance with him, if she took that step, the glass wouldn't break beneath her.

She cleared her throat. 'Did you go up the Burj Khalifa?'

'Yes, I've been up there a few times actually, it's… incredible. There are so many skyscrapers in that city but they are all dwarfed by this monster of a building. It almost looks too tall to be real.'

'I'd love to see it one day,' Clover said.

'I'd love to take you.'

There was silence in the room and he knew he'd said the wrong thing. Where was the rule book for this? They were clearly all privy to what was going on but how could he play the game if he didn't know the rules?

'Did you pick up any more amazing t-shirts?' Aria said, papering over the cracks.

'Of course, I'm sure you'll see them over the next few days.'

'Don't encourage him,' Noah said. 'I've seen enough of those ridiculous t-shirts to last me a lifetime.'

Angel laughed. It was an ongoing joke between them that Noah would moan about how Angel dressed for work and that Angel never paid any attention to it.

'Now you're back, you can go down to the Halloween festival in the village and take some photos and videos,' Noah said.

'Yes, and at the hotel too,' Aria said. 'We're having a campfire in the gardens tomorrow night and we'll be roasting marshmallows. We need as many different photos as possible of all the events so we can showcase it on our website for next year.'

'Sure, no problem. It'll be good to see it all actually,' Angel said. He turned his attention to Clover. 'Maybe you can show me around.'

She smiled. 'I'd like that.'

He watched her, their eyes locked. She made him feel so warm inside.

'So you're back for a few months now?' Skye said, interrupting the moment between him and Clover.

He nodded, finishing the last of his pizza. 'I have no plans to go anywhere right now. It's good to be home.'

Clover looked up at the word 'home', studying him. He frowned. That word seemed odd even to his own ears. Because he'd travelled so much with Noah he hadn't had a proper home for several years. It had suited him fine – he'd got to see the world, meet wonderful people and, if he ever came back to the UK, he'd always stay with one of his sisters. It was funny that his mind had made the connection that the Sapphire Bay Hotel was his home. It was probably just because Noah was loved-up, content and making a life for himself here and it had rubbed off on Angel a little. He wasn't about to follow in his footsteps.

'It's good to be back, I mean,' Angel said.

'Home is where the heart is,' Jesse muttered. Although he probably hadn't intended everyone to hear, it was clear everyone had as they all looked at him.

Jesse blushed and Skye smiled, leaning her head against his shoulder.

Angel cleared his throat. 'Do you guys want to see some photos from Dubai?'

They all nodded and he fished his phone from his jeans.

The last thing he wanted was to make decisions with his heart.

Clover waved goodbye to her family and closed the door behind them. She paused for a moment and then turned round to face Angel. He was standing in the lounge, hands in his pockets, watching her. Her sisters had prolonged the evening until late into the night so she wouldn't have to be alone with him and she felt awful. She wasn't scared to be alone with him, she was making this into a much bigger deal than it really was. Now it was just them, he would definitely want to talk. And she was going to be brave and explain everything. Probably.

'Well, I'm still really tired,' Angel said. 'So I think I'll head up to bed.'

She frowned in confusion. 'I thought you wanted to talk.'

He cocked his head, surveying her. 'I don't think *you* want that.'

'Oh god, Angel, I do and I don't. Part of me wants a normal relationship with you but there's a big part of me that's terrified of it. And I don't know if I'm ready for that or if I'll ever be. I know things won't change unless I take that leap and I know I have to trust in you to catch me when I do, but it's going to take some time.'

He stared at her and she felt her heart plummet into her stomach.

'Please tell me that's what you wanted to talk to me about and it wasn't just that you wanted to show me some of your new silly t-shirts,' Clover said, her cheeks flaming. Had she completely misread this?

He smiled and then moved towards her. 'I absolutely wanted to talk to you about that, about us. But there's no rush for this, no deadline. I'll be on Jewel Island for the next few months. I have no doubt that at some point this will happen for us. When you're ready.'

He certainly had more faith in them than she did.

He bent his head and kissed her gently on the cheek, his soft touch on her skin making her heart sing. 'Goodnight Clover.'

Angel moved away and up the stairs and she listened to him moving around, brushing his teeth in the bathroom, and then a moment later she heard his bedroom door close.

She bit her lip, wondering if she should follow him up the stairs and tell him everything, but the thought of that made her feel sick.

Clover walked upstairs and changed for bed, feeling angry

and sad when, just a few hours before, she'd been so happy about his arrival. She washed her face and cleaned her teeth. She stared at herself in the mirror and didn't like what she saw, what she'd become. She hated this turmoil inside of her, this inability to move on with her life.

She made a decision. Tomorrow she would do something to change this. Maybe she'd tell him, or maybe she'd bypass that and just kiss him, which was a much more pleasurable thought. She wasn't sure yet, but it would be a step forward, not a step back.

With that decisive thought in her head, she turned and went to bed.

CHAPTER THREE

Clover had just finished her Zumba class the next day and was going through some of the plans for the upcoming Christmas wedding when there was movement at her office door.

Angel was there, leaning against the door frame and watching her with that lovely lazy half smile. It made her heart leap simply at the sight of him. Today he was wearing a t-shirt with a googly eyed pumpkin, which seemed very appropriate.

'So, Noah has asked me to go and take some pictures of the Halloween festival for the website. I wondered if you fancied coming down to the village with me this morning and showing me around? I don't want to miss anything.'

She looked at the work on her desk. She needed to get some of this preparation done for the wedding but she had a few weeks yet to get it all ready. She didn't want to turn down spending time with Angel alone again, it would look like she was avoiding him.

She stood up. 'I'd like that. It'll be busy down there as it's

Saturday but that will probably look good for the photos if there are lots of people enjoying themselves.'

'That's true – if something looks popular, more people will want to try it,' Angel said.

She grabbed her coat and walked out the office with him, ignoring the less than discreet thumbs up and exaggerated wink from Tilly as they made their way across reception together.

Sylvia O'Hare, one of their most eccentric elderly guests, was sitting in reception tapping away on her laptop. She was in her eighties, favoured a purple cloak and big crazy hats and she also wrote very successful erotic fiction. She had a huge Pyrenean Mountain Dog called Snowflake lying at her feet.

'Are you two lovebirds off to the Halloween fair?'

Clover smiled and didn't bother to correct her. Sylvia had been dropping hints about Angel and Clover getting together for months. And it was slightly better than Tilly's attempts the day before. 'We are, have you been down there yet?'

'I went yesterday. It seems lovely for the children but a bit tame for me.'

'Oh, there's two parts to it, Sylvia. The daytime is for the kids and families. The night-time is for the adults. You should pop down tonight and see what happens after dark. It's quite creepy.'

'Well I do love to be scared. I'll have to take a look after dinner.'

Clover and Angel walked out of the hotel. The sun was shining, the sky a beautiful pale denim blue, but there was a definite nip in the air. There had been a frost that morning and some of the leaves and grass still sparkled with that sugar-coated sheen.

Clover slipped her coat on as they walked through the hotel gardens and over the headland that would take them to the little village. She pulled Angel to a stop next to an old oak tree as the village appeared beneath them: the colourful painted houses and the flurry of activity down the high street and across the village green as everyone enjoyed the fair.

'This is my favourite spot on the island. You can see almost the whole of Jewel Island from up here, the houses, the shops, the beaches, hills and meadows. Jade Harbour with its array of different boats. The animals grazing up on the fields. When I was a kid, I used to climb this tree with my little telescope and watch the villagers for hours. It used to fascinate me, watching them go about their lives, going to the shops, stopping to have a chat on the street, playing on the beach. It was like watching a movie. We were always a little bit removed from the village up here in the hotel and this way, watching them, it made me feel connected to them.'

'Wow,' Angel laughed. 'You were a nosy neighbour.'

Clover laughed. 'I know. My telescope wasn't that strong, I couldn't see inside the houses or anything like that, just outside on the village street. They had no idea I was watching them and it kind of felt like a big secret. No one knew I was doing it. Until my dad caught me one day.'

'Oh no, were you in trouble?'

Clover laughed. 'No, he actually built me that old tree-house so I could watch them more safely.'

Angel laughed as he looked up at the ramshackle old hut, buried deep amongst the branches of the ancient oak. 'He aided and abetted.'

Clover nodded. 'Yes and he encouraged me to take notes.'

Angel laughed loudly. 'What kind of notes?'

'I had a whole book. Mrs Gillespie went into the butchers at 10.02 a.m., she came out 10.37 with no bags.'

'Oh my god, was she having an affair?'

'Looking back, it's highly likely, but I had no idea what I was recording back then.'

Angel looked back up at the treehouse. 'So this is where little Clover spent her childhood?'

'Yes, I loved it. It had this big red, squashy rug on the floor, a couple of brightly coloured beanbags. I used to take my little battery-powered radio up there, and just listen. Sometimes, in my teens, I'd even take boys up there. We'd have a little kiss and talk about movies. Life was so much simpler back then.'

Angel smiled. 'Have you been up there recently?'

'Oh god, no. I left here not long after I was eighteen to go to university and of course I came back to visit often but not to live. I haven't been up there since before I left. I doubt it's even safe now.'

Angel looked up. 'It looks pretty sturdy. How did you get up?'

'There was a rope ladder on a pulley, Dad was quite good at rigging up that sort of thing. Although the whole ladder came down when I was sixteen or seventeen. I kind of stopped going up there after that.'

'So your stuff could still be up there, the rug, your notebook of the secret life of the Jewel Island villagers?'

'I doubt it's still up there, I presume the weather has ravished it. I'm not even sure I kept the notebook there, I know I'd take it back to the hotel sometimes.'

'We have to take a look,' Angel insisted.

'Well, if we can find a decent ladder we can come back here one day. Come on, I want to show you the fair.'

An icy gust blew around them, causing the fallen leaves to swirl and flutter. Clover pulled her coat around her more tightly as they walked down towards the village.

'It must feel a lot colder here than in Dubai.'

'Oh yes, the last month or so has been scorching over

there. It'd just started to turn a bit cooler in the last few weeks but it was still thirty-five degrees when I left.'

'Thirty-five is cooler?' Clover laughed.

'Yes, it'd been so much hotter than that. It's literally built in a desert so, yeah, it's that dry kind of heat. So actually this coolness is really refreshing. I love autumn though, it's my favourite time of year. The colours are so beautiful and it feels like it's time to hunker down for the winter.'

'I love it too, cosy fires and hot chocolates, that feeling that things are changing. I like that. It's like starting again.'

They were silent for a while. 'What would you like to change, one thing that you'd love to change the most?' Angel asked.

Clover thought for a moment but there was only one thing she wanted to change about her life. She couldn't change her past but she *was* in control of her future.

'I'd like to not be scared any more,' Clover said. 'If I could change one thing it would be that.'

Angel carried on walking, clearly deep in thought. 'And what is it you're scared of?'

God, how to sum it up in one sentence, because there was so much she was scared about. She was scared about telling Angel why she was holding back and him not wanting to deal with that baggage, scared of losing him when they hadn't even started a relationship. She was scared to put her trust in Angel for him to let her down. She was scared of betrayal and being humiliated. She was scared of never being able to move on and have a normal relationship again.

'I suppose I'm scared of love.'

Angel nodded, accepting this completely. 'Philophobia is the fear of falling in love. It's not that unusual, especially if you've had a traumatic incident.'

She stared at him. There was a name for it. That suddenly

made her feel a little better. She wasn't the only one who had been through this. Although her circumstances were possibly slightly more unique than others, it still boiled down to the same thing.

'Was there a traumatic incident?' Angel asked.

'Yeah, you could say that,' Clover said. She felt bad about keeping him in the dark, but she wasn't ready to talk about what had happened either.

To her surprise, Angel didn't push it any further, but he did slip his hand into hers again and it filled her heart. If she was ever going to move on, then Angel was definitely the best person to do that with. He was so patient and kind and she knew in her heart she could trust him.

She spotted Jesse and Skye a little way off, sitting under a tree together, cuddling and laughing.

'God, aren't they the perfect couple,' Clover said, glad of the distraction.

'Apart from that they're divorced,' Angel said.

'Yeah, apart from that.'

'What's their story anyway? Why did they get divorced?'

'Oh, it wasn't a real marriage. They were friends and they got married so she could stay in Canada while she got her working visas sorted. They agreed it would be for a year then they would divorce.'

'But they clearly love each other. Why not stay married when they realised it was more than just a marriage of convenience?'

'Jesse has sole custody of his daughter Bea. I think he didn't want to start anything serious because of her. He's an idiot, Skye absolutely adores her, and Bea loves Skye. But I think he was afraid of Bea getting hurt. So they divorced and now they have this weird no-strings-attached arrangement instead.'

Angel shook his head. 'Well, I guess it works for them. I

can't imagine if I ever loved someone as much as they clearly do that I would ever want to leave them, but then I don't have a daughter to think about so who am I to judge.'

Clover nodded. 'They seem happy enough this way.'

They walked down from the headland and into the village. Jewel Island had been transformed for Halloween: pumpkin bunting was strewn between the buildings and every shop and restaurant had wonderfully spooky displays of witches, skeletons and ghosts in every window. The whole village had pulled out all the stops. Her sister, Aria, had come up with the idea to hold a week-long festival to celebrate Halloween and everyone had embraced it with great gusto. There were little market stands in the street with Halloween games and activities: face painting, pumpkin carving and decorating, and pin the wart on the witch. The stall holders and shop owners were all in costumes and there were various scary stories being told by haggard old witches, creepy zombies and ghostly pirates.

Angel started taking loads of pictures and little mini videos as they made their way through the high street.

'Angel!' an excited voice rang out and Clover turned to see Izzy, the fifteen-year-old daughter of Delilah, one of the hotel receptionists. Izzy had worked at the hotel for a few weeks back in the spring when they were trying to get the hotel redecorated. She had teamed up with Angel on creating a renovation plan to show journalists and bloggers. Izzy was great at drawing and had helped to decorate Cones at the Cove with lots of ice cream and dessert related pictures too. Izzy had developed a little bit of a hero crush on Angel and it was easy to see why.

'Hey Izzy,' Angel smiled, easily.

'Hi Izzy,' Clover said.

Izzy immediately hugged Angel and he wrapped an arm around her shoulders.

Clover smiled. Izzy had grown so much in confidence over the last six months from the shy girl who had initially come to ask for work and she wondered if Angel had played any part in that growth.

'You're back! How long are you back for?' Izzy asked.

'A few months at least.'

'How was Dubai?'

'It was brilliant. You on half term this week?'

'Yes, me and my friends are going to camp for a few nights up by Moonstone Lake, no parents, just us.'

'Oh god, that is going to be trouble,' Angel laughed.

'Won't you be cold?' Clover asked.

'I have the thickest sleeping bag you've ever seen and we're taking duvets and blankets with us, so I'm sure we'll be fine. We have a gas stove and we're going to make ourselves hot chocolates every night and bacon sandwiches every morning.'

'Sounds like you have it all in hand,' Angel said. 'You enjoying the festivities?'

Clover smiled. He was so good with Izzy. He was in no rush to move away, just happy to chat to her for as long as she needed.

'Yes it's fab, but it's better at night.'

'I'll have to come down and take a look.'

'Yes you should. Oh, Dawn is waiting for me, I have to go. It's good to have you back!'

Izzy rushed off and Angel turned his attention back to Clover.

'You have such a lovely way with her,' Clover said.

'Oh, I have four younger sisters, so it comes naturally.'

They'd talked about his sisters before, but she hadn't realised how many he had.

'Wow! Four is a lot growing up in one household. I thought it was bad with two, I can't imagine four. We would always steal each other's clothes and make-up and fight like cat and dog, but then be best friends again a few minutes later. Plus all those female hormones flying about, I don't know how my poor dad coped.'

'Well, fortunately, they didn't really steal my clothes too often – apart from my hoodies, they were always going missing. I was nine when Mum met and married my stepdad and then started popping out daughters like it was some kind of hobby. "I've finished another painting, oh and I'm pregnant, again."'

Clover laughed.

'Eliza was only two weeks old when Mum fell pregnant with Emily. They were in the same class at school. Everyone thought they must be twins. They looked the same too, carbon copies of one another.

'I adored them,' he smiled fondly. 'I'd been on my own for so long, just me and my mum. Everyone thought I'd find it hard to adjust, that I'd resent them, but it was wonderful being big brother to these four, bold, colourful little girls. They were into everything. Mum was always a fairly tidy person and all that went out the window when she had four little girls under the age of five. There were toys everywhere.'

'I bet there was a lot of pink,' Clover said.

'Oh god yes. And glitter too; I remember finding glitter in my clothes, on my face, in my hair for years. Where does it all come from?'

Clover laughed. 'Don't you know that girls are born with glitter in their veins?'

'That explains a lot.'

'I bet they loved having you as an older brother.'

'We were very close. I was so protective of them. God, when Aurelia started dating, I actually followed her on a date once, she had no idea I was there. But the boy she was with had a bit of a reputation of sleeping around and I wanted to make sure he didn't get too carried away with her. Mum gave me such a telling-off when she found out. She was a lot more laid-back than I was when it came to the girls. God knows what I'd be like if I ever had kids of my own, I think I'd carry them around in bubble wrap for the first twenty years.'

'Yes, I always hoped I'd be the cool, laid-back mum, but I'd probably be over the top and completely overprotective too. I think Delilah has done a wonderful job with Izzy, being a single mum and all. I'm not sure I'd be letting my kid go camping with no adults at the age of fifteen – maybe when they were twenty-five I'd be more agreeable to it.'

Angel laughed and glanced over at Izzy who was playing a game at a nearby stall. 'She reminds me a lot of Rose actually, or at least how Rose used to be – she's grown up a bit since then. She's talking of coming here for New Year's actually. She will adore you.'

Clover couldn't help but smile at that. It was such a casual comment but she loved that Angel wanted to introduce her to his sister. It felt significant, somehow, like she was important enough to meet his family, even if they were just friends.

'I'd love to meet her,' Clover said.

CHAPTER FOUR

'Fancy a go at apple bobbing?' Clover gestured to one of the stalls where there appeared to be a ghost in charge of the activity, a lady dressed all in grey, with a grey face and silvery-white long hair.

Angel grinned. 'Of course, but let's make it interesting. Whoever takes the longest to get the apple has to buy one of those creepy-looking treats from the food stalls for the other person.'

'Oh you're so on,' Clover said. 'I am an expert at this.'

They walked over to see a huge barrel filled with a bright red liquid and apples bobbing around inside. Clover paid and Angel moved around to one side of the barrel while Clover moved to the other.

'Hands behind your back,' the ghost said. Clover and Angel did as they were told. 'Three, two, one, go.'

Clover and Angel immediately ducked their heads trying to catch an apple that just slipped away from them as soon as they touched it. Clover couldn't help giggling as she chased her apple around the top of the barrel and laughing at Angel who was trying to do the same. Just as she seemed to be getting hold of one, he knocked it out the way. In revenge she deliberately dunked an apple and it sprang up and hit Angel in the face, splashing him with the red liquid. He let out a bark of a laugh and continued trying to knock the apples out her way rather than trying to capture his own.

Eventually, she managed to pin one apple against the side but as she took a bite, Angel took a bite of her apple too. As she started to bring her apple up, Angel clung onto it as well.

Clover let it go, laughing so much. 'You're such a big cheat.'

'Some might say it was resourceful or strategic.'

'More like sneaky.'

Angel shrugged. 'I'd call that a win.'

'I'd call that a draw,' Clover protested.

'Fine, I'll buy you a treat of your choice and you can buy me one.'

'OK, deal.'

The food stalls had an amazing selection of gorgeous Halloween treats. There were cake pops decorated as eyeballs, meringue ghosts, gingerbread skeletons, beautifully iced cookies and cakes and strawberries dipped in coloured chocolate and adorned with spooky faces. There were dead man's fingers, which were essentially just churros with a red chocolate sauce, and various doughnuts in Halloween designs. For those who preferred savoury foods there were cheese spiders, mummy sausage rolls, bat-shaped sandwiches and monster mini pizzas.

'Come on, I'll let you buy me one of those cupcakes.' Clover pointed to a cake stand, recognising Kendra, the owner of the village bakery, dressed as a mummy.

'These cakes look great,' Clover said as they drew close. They were all so beautifully decorated with various Halloween paraphernalia.

'Thank you, I had a lot of fun making them,' Kendra said, her eyes flitting between the two of them with curiosity and delight.

Clover smiled. 'Have you two met? This is my friend Angel, he's Noah's assistant, and this is Kendra, the world's best baker.'

'We have met a few times,' Kendra said. 'But I haven't seen you down in the village for a while.'

'I've been away in Dubai with work for the last five or six weeks, but it's good to be back. And if these cakes are the kind of thing you sell in your bakery on a regular basis, I can see I'll definitely have to come down to the village more often.'

'Oh, you're a charmer,' Kendra laughed.

Clover picked up a cake that had a marshmallow ghost on the top and Angel chose one that looked like the Cookie Monster eating a large cookie.

After Angel had paid, they moved away, under Kendra's watchful eye.

'Isn't she your godmother?' Angel asked when they were out of hearing distance.

'Yes, but she moved away to London when I was really young, maybe five. Aria would have been eleven, so I don't really have any memory of her when I was growing up like Aria does. Aria even stayed in touch with her while she was away. Kendra came back around five or six years ago, but I'd already left Jewel Island then. So I know her as much as I know the other islanders but I wouldn't say we are close like she is with Aria.'

'Ah, that makes sense. I hear Aria talk about Kendra quite a bit, but you don't really, other than how lovely her cakes are.'

Clover took a bite. 'They really are very lovely.'

They walked through the stalls a bit more.

'Oh look, you can make your own toffee apples,' Angel

pointed.

'Oh yes, great idea.'

They wandered over and, after Angel had paid, they were both given apples on sticks and directed to a number of trays and pots of different toppings. There was white chocolate to make ghost apples, orange chocolate to make pumpkins and even black chocolate to make spiders. There were plenty of eyeballs to choose from too, plus gummy worms and other toppings. There were several very artistic examples to demonstrate the kinds of things they could make and though Clover had no idea about Angel's artistic ability, she thought it was pretty safe to say that their apples would look nothing like them.

'OK, I'm definitely going to kick your ass this time,' Angel said, taking a few photos of the finished apples.

Clover turned to Seamus, the village mayor, who was dressed as Frankenstein's monster. 'Can you be the judge, who does the best apple?'

Seamus laughed. 'When the kids ask me whose is the best, I always say they are all beautiful, but I don't mind being brutally honest with you two. I think you can take it.'

'I can, I'm not sure about Angel,' Clover said, grabbing her apple and dunking it into the white chocolate.

'Hey, are we starting already?'

'Well if you're going to kick my ass, I better get a shift on.'

Angel grabbed his apple and, using a knife, cut a small slit in the side. Clover watched him in confusion for a moment before returning her attention to her own apple.

She dipped a cocktail stick into the black chocolate and started drawing lines around the apple in an attempt to make a spider's web but it didn't really work out as planned. The white chocolate was too warm and the black chocolate just merged into it so the whole thing started to look grey. She glanced over at Angel who had dumped his apple in the red chocolate and was now creating some kind of face.

Changing her mind about the spider's web, she decided to try some kind of mummy look instead. She grabbed two eyes and stuck them to the side, then took a few thick strings of candy shoelaces and wrapped them around the apple. It looked quite effective.

'OK, I'm done,' Angel said, turning his apple towards her. The slit he'd cut out earlier had now been filled with marshmallow teeth and he'd also managed to do green chocolate eyes. She had to admit, if she were judging, Angel's would win. Hers kind of looked like a five-year old had made it.

'Seamus, what do you think?'

Seamus studied both apples, clearly taking his role as judge very seriously. 'The winner is...' he said dramatically. 'Angel's.'

'Damn it,' Clover said.

Angel looked at hers. 'What were you trying to do?'

'It was going to be a spider's web.'

He squinted his eyes. 'Really?'

'Not now, it's more of a zombie mummy instead. It's abstract.'

'It is that.'

Clover laughed. 'You're so rude.'

'You two can leave your apples here to set if you want. I have a fridge under here, you can collect them in around fifteen minutes.'

'Perfect,' Clover said.

Angel slung an arm around her shoulders. 'Come on, I'll take you on the ghost train to make up for your lack in apple-decorating skills.'

'Thanks Seamus. Will we see you at the campfire tonight?'

'Yes, definitely, we wouldn't miss it.'

Clover moved away from the stall, saying her goodbyes to

Seamus who gave her a wink as they walked off together. She was sure a lot of the villagers would have something to say about her and Angel being together if they thought they were now a couple.

'What's this?' Angel said, pointing to a poster that advertised the upcoming dance show. She'd been hoping she could get away without him finding out about that.

When Seamus had suggested the children of the village might want to put on a Halloween dance show and Clover had told him she thought it was a wonderful idea, she'd had no idea that he would take that to mean she would co-ordinate and choreograph it all. And while she was very happy to teach children to dance for fun, she'd never put on or been part of any kind of show before. She had been practising with the children for weeks for what would be a five-minute performance, but she didn't feel any more ready for it than when she'd started.

To make matters worse, she and the children would be dressed up in ridiculous costumes. She definitely didn't need Angel to see that.

'Are you involved in this?' Angel said.

Clover cleared her throat. 'It's a kids' show. Probably not your thing.'

'Oh, I don't know about that. Children are always entertaining.'

'There's pig racing too, think it's at the same time, that's probably much more up your street.'

'Now that does sound like fun,' Angel said.

Hoping that would be enough to distract him from the dance show, she quickly changed the subject. 'We need to try one of those pancakes later,' she pointed over to one of the stands. 'They are supposed to be amazing. I think I'd like the Toblerone one or maybe the salted caramel or both.'

'Well I certainly want to get the full experience of the fair,' Angel said, obviously taking his pancake-eating responsibilities very seriously.

They carried on through the village. At the end of the street, on the village green, there was a Halloween-themed funfair with spooky rides, but it was the haunted house and ghost train that were proving most popular. Like the whole festival, these rides were tamer in the daytime and would be ramped up with the scare factor at night.

'This place looks great,' Angel said, looking around and taking photos.

'The funfair is an outside job, obviously, and some of the stall holders have come from off the island too, but most of it has all been put together by the villagers. Aria made it clear that if the hotel was doing their bit by redecorating and renovating to get more tourists to come to the island, we had to give them something to stay here for. And your advertisements for the festival were brilliant, they really helped to get people through our doors.'

'I'm going to make sure I get loads of videos and photos over the coming week so we can advertise it properly next year. I didn't have a lot of things to show for the adverts this time, so I just made a few spooky trailers and hoped it would do the job.'

'It did, we are sold out for the entire week.'

'So is there anything else going on apart from this and the dance show?'

'Well you need to come down here at night too, the scare factor is definitely turned up after dark. There are a few mini events. Noah is having a campfire in the hotel gardens tonight, well several fires actually, there'll be marshmallows and s'mores and other snacks. That should be fun. There's the dance show and pig racing on Monday, there's pumpkin carving too. There's a zombie run on Thursday and a pumpkin treasure trail on Friday and a lantern walk through the gardens on Friday night. A week tomorrow, on Halloween night, there's also a big ball up at the hotel. It's fancy dress so it should be a good laugh.'

'I'll definitely need to come along and video that.'

'You could come with me if you want,' Clover said, looking away and trying to make it sound suitably vague.

He paused to look at her. 'As a date?'

Clover focussed her attention on picking bits of chocolate off her fingers. 'As... two friends who like each other very much.'

'I'll take that,' Angel said. 'I'd very much like to take you to the ball.'

Clover smiled. It was a start. And maybe, at some point between now and then, she could pluck up the courage to tell him why she was holding back.

The queue for the ghost train was quite big so they veered off to go to the haunted house instead.

'So what are we going to see in here?' Angel said.

'There are actors that will jump out on us as we walk around, although it's a slightly calmer version right now. You'll have to come back down here one night to get the full experience.'

They paid to go in and Angel slipped his hand into hers as they stepped through into the darkness.

'Are you protecting me or are you wanting me to protect you?' Clover said.

He stroked a finger down her face. 'Maybe we can look after each other.'

She smiled, hoping he was talking about more than just the haunted house.

CHAPTER FIVE

Clover picked up a marshmallow and skewered it on a stick, holding it over the flames until it turned a golden brown. Next to her Skye seemed to be going for an extra-black coating while Aria was merely warming her marshmallow, rather than waiting for it to go gooey.

Clover looked around the garden where there were fairy lights strewn between the trees. Noah had organised little firepits dotted around the lawn with comfy outdoor seats and thick soft blankets for the guests to cuddle under. There was a man from the village serving roasted chestnuts, another selling hot cider and hot fruit drinks for the kids, while others were selling popcorn and cakes. They didn't have a huge selection of stands, just a few to make the setting seem more intimate rather than commercial.

Many of the villagers had come up to enjoy the campfires at the hotel too, maybe to escape the noise and buzz of the evening activities in the village. Seamus and his wife Kathy were laughing over how their s'mores were breaking up. Tilly's husband, Ben, was carefully bouncing their baby boy,

Joshua, in his papoose as Tilly roasted marshmallows for them both. Kendra and her new boyfriend, Phillippe, were cuddled together under blankets looking very loved-up and cosy. Delilah and her daughter Izzy were laughing and chatting as they assembled their s'mores. It made Clover smile. In the past there had been a slight animosity from the villagers towards the hotel because the islanders felt the hotel had let them down; tourists had stopped coming because the hotel had been in such a bad state and that had impacted on the businesses of the island too. But now that the tourists were flooding into the island again, it felt like the hotel was a much-valued member of the community once more. Aria had made it very clear that it worked both ways, that if the hotel was doing its bit to support the island, then the islanders had to do their bit to support the hotel, so it was nice to see so many of them there that night.

Clover sat back on her chair and pulled the blanket around her, Skye snuggled in next to her, picking apart her black marshmallow and putting the crispy skin in her mouth. Aria slid a strawberry onto her kebab stick and then sat back too. Clover pulled the blanket round Aria's shoulders. The fire was doing a good job in stopping most of the chill of the autumn night but there was a definite need for the blankets too.

Across the fire, Angel, Jesse and Noah were also roasting marshmallows and making s'mores as they laughed and chatted about something that Clover couldn't quite hear.

'How's everything going with him?' Aria asked, gesturing with her marshmallow kebab in Angel's direction.

Clover smiled. 'Good. He's a lovely man. I actually managed to pluck up the courage to ask him to the ball next Sunday and he said yes.'

'Like a date?' Skye said.

'Um, sort of. Yes, I guess.' She saw her sisters exchange

glances. 'Don't look like that, I plan to tell him what he's dealing with before we get that far. And he's already said he's happy to wait to talk about it until I'm ready, he's not going to push me on that. He's been really patient and understanding. And I'm just enjoying being with him right now. We spent most of the morning at the fair and it was lovely to spend some time with him without any pressure for it to be something more or for me to bare my soul to him. I'm psyching myself up to scaring him away with all my issues.'

'I really don't think that will happen,' Aria said.

Clover glanced across the fire at Angel and realised he was watching her with a smile. It made her feel warm inside. 'Yeah, maybe you're right. How are things going with you and the adoption anyway, it all seems to have gone quiet on that front?'

She knew that her sister and Noah had been going through the adoption process for months now. There had been so much paperwork and so many hoops to jump through that it didn't seem like it would ever happen. As Aria had been adopted by their parents when she was a baby, adoption had always been something she'd wanted to do for another child, and, with Noah growing up in foster care, Clover knew how important this was to both of them.

'It has gone quiet,' Aria said. 'But apparently that's fairly normal. These things take time. They have everything they need now, they have our medical history, the lovely references you two and Angel wrote for us. We've met social workers, had preparation classes, we've met with other parents trying to adopt and ones that have successfully. We had our entire history delved into, including whether we have any criminal records. All of our paperwork has now gone off to an adoption panel and they will make a recommendation to the agency whether we should be allowed to adopt or not. Our social worker is pretty confident we should hear back from them any day now.'

'I can't believe you're going to be parents,' Skye said, still attacking her marshmallow.

'If they say yes,' Aria said.

'They will, of course they will,' Clover said. 'Why would they possibly say no?'

'Well neither of us have any child experience. I don't have nieces or nephews and although Noah does, he doesn't really see his brother that often to have any kind of real relationship with them. There's lots of little things they could pick on if they were really looking for reasons not to say yes. And I don't blame them for being extra critical. This is a child's life we're talking about, they have to know, a hundred and ten percent, that any child they place with us is going to the best possible home.'

'They will look at you and Noah and know straightaway that the child is going to have the best parents in the world,' Clover said.

Skye nodded. 'The rest of it is just box-ticking, but I guarantee they will say yes. I told them how good you were with Bea.'

'You did?' Aria said.

'Bea adores you, both of you. She loves coming here as she gets completely spoiled rotten by you two. You're great with her.'

Clover smiled at her twin. 'I think she loves coming here, mainly because she gets to spend time with you. You're part of her family even if technically you're not.'

Skye looked wistfully across the fire at Jesse. 'I would give anything to have that life back. I don't think I'm ever going to have children of my own, but bringing Bea up, watching her grow in that year I was with them, was the best year of my life.'

Clover finished her marshmallow, her heart aching for Skye. She had married ridiculously young to a man called Oliver who had been desperate for children. Three tragic miscarriages and a year later, they had divorced. It wasn't something they ever really talked about as Skye had firmly drawn a line under that part of her life. But Clover hated that Skye had given up on ever having children and with this weird long distance, friends with benefits arrangement with Jesse, it didn't seem like she would ever move on and have the chance to have a proper family of her own.

'You could adopt too,' Clover said gently. 'You don't have to close the door on that part of your life.'

'I could,' Skye said. 'It is something I've thought about with everything that Aria has gone through over the last few months. Maybe one day.'

Clover sighed sadly. She knew Skye was clinging onto the vain hope that one day she and Jesse would get back together and until that happened, or Skye accepted that it was never going to happen, she would never really move on.

'What about you?' Skye said, shifting the attention away from her. 'Do you not want that life too?'

Clover let out a heavy breath. 'That feels very far away right now.'

She'd had so many hopes and dreams about her relationship with Marcus but those dreams had been crushed in a blink of an eye and it was hard to ever imagine wanting that life with anyone now. It was safer to avoid anything serious or any kind of commitment, that way she could never get hurt.

～

Clover watched Angel, sitting in the armchair in her lounge. He looked happy and content here. They'd come back to her cottage after the campfire, chatted for a while and then put a movie on.

They were watching one of those romantic comedies where the characters are pretty much guaranteed the happy ending, no matter what mishaps and mayhem they went through in the rest of the film. Love always won out. There was no room for emotionally abusive assholes in these kinds of films. The 'bad guys' in these films might be a woman who had her sights set on the hero, thwarting the heroine's attempts at love, or some big businessman who was ruining the little village shop with his big department store. There was no one like Marcus in these films, no one who could ruin someone's life so completely in a mere matter of seconds.

The perfect happy ending for Clover seemed like an impossible dream right now.

Angel had not made any attempt to talk to her about what was holding her back and she liked that. He had even sat down on the armchair when she took the sofa, leaving a respectful distance, although she liked that a bit less. Throughout the film, she had been tempted to go and cuddle up to him, but she hadn't. She had no idea why she had been so worried about being alone with him the night before. He had been utterly lovely all day, as he always was. That was part of the reason she'd started falling for him in the first place, because in her heart she knew she could trust him. She had taken a small step forward today, asking him to the ball, but maybe she needed to take another step. Although she had no idea what that step should be. It was too late in the day for deep, long conversations and Angel was clearly flagging.

The film came to an end and Angel turned his attention to

her. 'Well, today has been great fun. What exciting plans do we have for tomorrow?'

She smiled; she loved his enthusiasm. 'The fair will still be going on, so lots to see, but no special events.'

'Is the dance show not tomorrow?'

She narrowed her eyes. She wondered if he knew she was involved in that or at least suspected she was.

'That's actually the day after tomorrow. That and the pig racing are both happening Monday. I think the pig racing will be a lot of fun,' she said, trying to distract him from the dance show.

He smirked and she couldn't help smiling too. He'd definitely just seen straight through her distraction techniques. In fact, she'd flagged up the dance show even more.

'I have a wedding shoot tomorrow to oversee,' Clover quickly hurried on. 'We're mocking up a fake wedding for the website.'

'That's a great idea to do that,' Angel said, letting her change the subject. 'People want to see what their wedding will look like if they hold it here. It should drum up some business once people see the beauty of the island. I might follow the photographer around and take some photos of my own.' He stretched and yawned. 'Right, I think I'll go to bed.'

He made a move towards the stairs, paused and then bent his head and kissed her on the cheek. She smiled and opened her mouth to speak, to say something, but she had no idea what she wanted to say.

He squeezed her hand and walked up the stairs. She heard him moving around getting ready for bed and then she heard the bedroom door close.

She went upstairs, changed into her pyjamas and started cleaning her teeth.

She remembered what they'd talked about earlier that day,

that the one thing she wanted to change was to stop being scared. That change had to come from her, it wasn't going to come from Angel when he was being so bloody respectful and patient.

She thought about what he'd said the night before about needing to face his fears, pushing himself out of his comfort zone, and she knew she had to do the same. She made a snap decision. She quickly walked to his bedroom door and knocked before she could change her mind.

There was a silence for a moment and then Angel's wary voice. 'Come in.'

She walked in and quickly closed the door behind her, leaning against it. The room was in semi darkness, the open curtains letting moonlight pour through. Angel was lying in bed, the duvet around his waist. His arms were tanned and strong and she realised this was the first time she'd seen him without a top on. He was utterly divine.

He didn't say a word, his eyes filled with unending patience as he waited for her.

'I decided I wanted to try something that scared me.'

'OK,' Angel said, carefully.

'Can I stay here tonight?'

Angel stared at her and for an awful moment she thought he might say no, but the next thing he lifted up the duvet for her. She hesitated. It suddenly felt like a big step, when in reality it wasn't at all. *Be brave*, he'd said before. She walked towards the bed and quickly climbed in by his side. Lying on her back and staring at the ceiling, she felt tense. But he didn't make a move towards her and she liked that. Marcus had never been able to keep his hands off her in bed and at first she'd enjoyed it but towards the end of their short-lived relationship it kind of felt like he thought sex was his right.

She started to relax a little and then she felt Angel's hand slide across the bed towards her. To her surprise he took her hand, entwining his fingers with hers.

'We've got this, Clover Philips,' he said gently.

She smiled and felt herself relax even more. She shuffled closer and put her head on his chest. After a second he wrapped an arm around her and she closed her eyes. He was right, they were going to be OK.

CHAPTER SIX

When Angel walked through the hotel gardens the next day, the sky was the palest blue but the temperature was definitely a lot colder than it had been the day before. There was an icy wind that whipped off the beach and tore through the gardens, making the leaves rustle on the trees and dance in the sky like confetti. It was Sunday morning and no one was around to appreciate the beauty of the autumn gardens, most of the hotel guests were probably down in the village enjoying the fair. Stephen, the hotel gardener, was tending to the dahlias, which looked stunning as they fluttered in the autumn breeze in an array of brightly jewelled colours. The sunflowers and roses were all in full bloom too. As Angel drew closer to the hotel he could see the firepits were still out in the gardens after the night before. The guests had enjoyed sitting around making s'mores and roasting marshmallows and Noah had suggested they might hold another campfire night later in the week.

Angel's thoughts turned to Clover and how beautiful she'd looked the night before, sitting opposite him, the light of the fire making her face glow and her hair shine. Lying in bed with her last night had been utterly perfect. He hadn't wanted anything more from her, it had been enough to simply hold her in his arms. But then he'd woken that morning when it was still dark and found that she'd already gone. She'd taken a huge step the night before lying in bed with him but she'd clearly woken up that morning and decided it was a step too far.

He wanted to help her through this, but not knowing what *this* was made it very difficult to try and make better or, in fact, avoid making worse.

He knew Clover was dealing with something big and a hundred worst-case scenarios had already raced through his head but he had no idea which one it was or if he was even close.

Because she'd woken up that morning and regretted simply sleeping in the same bed, he was now doubting himself. He just wasn't sure he was the best man for the job of helping her move on. He adored her and it would kill him if he did anything to hurt her. But he'd never had a serious girlfriend in his life and, despite what Clover had said to her sisters about wanting something fun, this felt like something serious. He just didn't know if he had that in him.

But backing out now wasn't an option either. She was slowly unlocking the fortress she'd built around her and he couldn't walk away from that. It would hurt her and send her scuttling back inside her shell again just when she was venturing out.

He would take his lead from her on this one and if she thought she couldn't have a relationship with him after all, then maybe he could support her as a friend, if nothing else. Maybe he could help her find someone else to move on with, someone far more suitable. He ignored the ache in his chest at that thought.

~

Clover had just sat down in her office after two back-to-back dance lessons. She had a lot of work to do today, especially with the wedding shoot. Thankfully some of the staff had already helped dress certain areas of the hotel ready for the fake wedding. They'd cornered off one area of the restaurant, adding flowers and confetti to one of the tables, and hired a fake flower archway from the florist in the village which was currently situated in the garden. The photographer was already here, looking at all the different locations around the hotel, and the models and the hairdresser were going to arrive there soon. Clover really had to just oversee everything, but it was going to take a good chunk of her day.

Angel suddenly appeared in her doorway wearing another Halloween-themed t-shirt, this one had a flamingo wearing a witch's hat and riding on a broomstick.

'Hey,' Clover said, logging into her emails.

'I woke up this morning and you'd gone,' he said.

'I had a dance class.'

That was true but what was also true was that she'd woken up wrapped in his arms and panicked ever so slightly. She was scared of putting her trust in someone again, of becoming intimate with them, of putting herself in a position to be vulnerable again. She'd got up and quickly washed, dressed and left for the hotel while the sun was still thinking about rising. If Angel had woken up when it was still semi dark, he would know that she'd freaked out. She only hoped he'd woken at a decent time.

He smiled and something told her he had totally woken up early.

'No worries. Mind if I join you? I have work to do and it'd be good if I could pinch a corner of your desk.'

'Of course.'

She watched him sit down and get himself settled with his laptop. He really wasn't going to push her at all about this. Her heart swelled a little because of that.

She turned her attention to her emails. There were three in quick succession from the modelling agency.

She clicked on the first one and her heart sank. She quickly clicked on the next two to see if it got any better, but it didn't.

'Crap!'

Angel looked up from his laptop. 'What's up?'

'I'd booked all these models to come and mock up a wedding this afternoon, for our brochure and website, and they've just cancelled.'

'What? Did they give a reason?'

'Their van has broken down and they have no way of getting here. What are we going to do?'

'Are there no other modelling agencies nearby or slightly further afield?' Angel said.

'I don't know, and it's Sunday so I doubt there'd be any that could come today or even if there'd be anyone in the office to take the call. The photographer is already here, he costs a fortune, we can't cancel him. We've hired clothes, flowers, we even have a fake cake.'

'OK,' Angel said, slowly as he thought. 'Someone else then, someone from the village perhaps. We'd only really need a bride and groom. I'm sure we could get some wedding guests together easily enough, but the main focus will be the bride and groom looking loved-up in different parts of the hotel. We just need a couple that will look happy and in love.'

She thought about this, it could work.

'We also want someone who will fit into the wedding clothes we hired. The dress is a size ten – the model was an eight but it was all we could get and we were going to pin her into it.'

'What size are you?'

'Ten but I'm not doing it.'

'Why not?'

'Because I was hoping to have someone glamorous and gorgeous.'

His eyebrows shot up. 'Clover, you're one of the most beautiful women I've ever met.'

Oh god, this man. The way he looked at her, the things he said, made her feel so good about herself.

'Thank you.'

He shrugged. 'It's the truth. I know you don't see it but it's the truth.'

'I suppose I could do it. We have a hairdresser coming in shortly to do the bride's hair. I suppose if she can do something glamorous with my hair and the photographer doesn't get too close, we could get away with it. But only if you'll be my groom.'

He smiled. 'Are you asking me to marry you, Clover Philips?'

'Do *you* want to marry me?'

'I'd like that very much.'

She stared at him. This had suddenly taken a very serious turn.

Angel cleared his throat, possibly realising he'd pushed it too far. 'OK, what size is the suit?'

Clover checked the email from the agent to see the sizes. 'Thirty-eight.'

'Hmm, I'm a forty, forty-two.'

'Oh.' She surveyed his chest. He was huge and all muscle. Squeezing him into a suit several inches too small was probably not a good look.

'But fortunately, I do have my own tux that I keep for special events like hotel launches or parties. I could wear that.'

'That would work.'

'Well in that case, I shall marry you.'

Clover glanced up at movement in the doorway. Skye was standing there, her eyes wide. 'Well that escalated quickly. Angel only got here two days ago and now you're getting married?'

Clover laughed. 'My models have cancelled for the wedding shoot. Me and Angel are going to play at being bride and groom instead.'

'Oh, that could be fun. And not the worst reason to get married. My experience of marrying my best friend for immigration reasons didn't turn out too badly,' Skye said.

Apart from her sister ending up with a broken heart when Jesse had divorced her a year later as per their original agreement, Clover thought.

'I was just popping by to ask about the wedding shoot,' Skye said. 'Did you want to take some photos down in Cones at the Cove? We could get some cute shots of you two sharing an ice cream or a milkshake and it could help to showcase the café too.'

'That's a great idea, I'll add it to my list.'

Delilah, one of the receptionists poked her head round the door. 'Clover, the hairdresser is here.'

Clover stood up. 'Right, I should go and beautify myself.'

'I better go back to your cottage and dig out my suit,' Angel said.

'I'll see you back here in half hour.'

57

'Isn't it bad luck for the bride and groom to see each other before the wedding?'

She smiled. 'We don't need luck, we've got this.'

Angel was waiting in reception a while later trussed up to the nines in his tux. He didn't wear this kind of get-up a lot, he was much more comfortable in his jeans and one of his funky t-shirts.

Noah walked out of his office and then did a double-take when he saw him.

'I know I've been on at you to wear something smarter to work for the last few years, but this seems to be taking it a step too far,' Noah said.

'I think I could totally pull this off on a daily basis,' Angel said.

'It's certainly a step up from those ridiculous t-shirts you insist on wearing.'

Angel smiled. Noah didn't really care what Angel wore to work as his assistant, although he liked to moan about it.

'Clover's models for the wedding shoot let her down, I'm stepping in to help her.'

'Does that mean I have to put up with seeing your face on our website?'

'I'm afraid so,' Angel said.

'Who's the bride?'

'Clover.'

'Ah.'

'What's that mean?' Angel asked.

'I don't know, I just…' Noah trailed off.

Angel looked at him, expectantly.

'You're a decent bloke—'

'Jesus, a compliment, you feeling OK?'

'Shut up and listen. I'm just not sure it's a good idea for you to get involved with her.'

'And what does that mean?' Angel said, all humour now gone. It was one thing doubting his suitability for Clover, it was quite another for his friend to doubt him too.

'You're not known for your ability to make a commitment with a woman, are you? You're too afraid of standing still, of missing out on something wonderful in the world, to want to settle down for the rest of your life.'

Angel stared at Noah in surprise. They'd known each other for eight years and, despite Noah being his boss, they'd become very good friends but Angel had never realised that Noah knew him almost better than he knew himself.

'Clover is the kind of girl that needs forever,' Noah went on. 'Her last boyfriend was a dick and, despite what she says about wanting something casual, I think she needs someone who is there for the long run. I'm not sure if you want that.'

Angel had asked himself that question several times over the last few months because he'd never wanted to settle down, there was too much of the world left to explore. But there was something about Clover Philips that he just couldn't walk away from.

'I really don't think Clover wants something serious either,' Angel said. 'I think she just wants to date someone again, someone who isn't her ex. I don't want to do anything to hurt her, but I think we're both coming at this from the same page.'

'Look, just don't screw this up. I don't want to have to kick your ass,' Noah said and Angel laughed.

Just then Clover appeared at the top of the stairs, wearing a strapless silvery white dress that sparkled as she moved. Her hair was piled on top of her head in some elaborate plait and she was wearing what looked like a diamond necklace that glittered like stars. God, Angel had never seen anything as beautiful in his entire life. And, despite the fact that it was all fake and they weren't really getting married, he suddenly felt like the luckiest man in the world.

'Way to play it cool,' Noah said, quietly, and Angel quickly snapped his mouth shut.

Clover moved over to them. 'Do I look OK?'

Angel had no words at all, he could only stare at her.

'You look lovely,' Noah said, filling in the silence on Angel's behalf.

Angel nodded. 'You do.'

'I'll go and find the photographer,' Clover said, moving off.

Angel watched her go.

'Smooth,' Noah said, dryly.

Angel shook his head, he had to get it together.

CHAPTER SEVEN

Clover sighed.

Brian, the photographer, had already taken what felt like hundreds of photos, and her cheeks were aching from smiling so much. He'd taken pictures of them in various parts of the hotel, cutting the fake cake, sitting at the top table in the restaurant, having their first dance on the dance floor. It had been quite the attraction for some of the hotel guests and some of them evidently believed they were watching a real wedding. Even Sylvia had started taking pictures of her own, though Clover was quite sure she knew the truth. They'd been inside Skye's ice cream café, Cones at the Cove, and had photos sharing ice cream and they'd been outside in the gardens underneath the beautiful scarlet, amber and gold autumn leaves.

It had been slightly surreal having Angel holding her hand, standing close to her, having his arms around her. It had been wonderful of course, but more than a little bit odd. In between photos, he'd also lent her his jacket because the day was cold and a strapless dress was far from desirable for this kind of weather. Now they were having their photograph taken by the waterfall near her cottage. Brian was quite far away to try and get a long-distance shot and she and Angel had been under strict instructions to stand there next to the falls and look at each other lovingly.

'God, can you imagine really being a model if you have to do stuff like this? Brian has taken every photo from a million different angles,' Clover said, forcing a smile back onto her face, not knowing whether the photographer was zooming in to take some of the pictures.

'I know. Imagine if this really was our wedding day, we'd kind of lose the romance a little with the amount of photos he's taking.' Angel looked around. 'This place is magical though, I think he'll get some incredible shots and the autumn foliage is looking particularly dramatic. It would be good to do some more photos in the spring or summer to get some flowers and sunshine or if it snows but these will be an excellent start.'

She smiled. 'Are you asking to marry me again?'

'I could certainly get used to having you as my bride,' Angel said.

Her breath caught in her throat. That suddenly felt like a huge step forward even though Angel was completely joking. At some point she knew they would have the conversation about whether or not they were going to date, whether she was ready, and she'd have to tell him the truth. But the possibility of something serious like marriage scared her more than a little.

Brian came ambling over. 'OK, I think I've got almost everything I need and we've done all the places on the list. I think all we need now is a few photos of the kiss.'

Clover's heart leapt in her chest. Christ, she hadn't even thought about that.

Angel looked at her in concern and then started shaking his head. 'I don't think that's appropriate.'

Brian nodded emphatically. 'That's what everyone wants to see, trust me. When people get married that's what everyone gets excited about – when Wills and Kate got married and they kissed for the first time on the balcony, the crowd went wild. And when I show the finished photos to the bride and groom after the wedding, the first-kiss photo is the one they want to see the most.'

Clover eyed Angel. God she wanted to kiss him so badly, she'd thought about it so often over the last six months. But the last person she'd kissed had been her ex-boyfriend Marcus and he'd had been enough to put her off ever getting romantically involved with a man again. Could she really kiss Angel?

But Brian didn't exactly want a full-blown passionate embrace, he just wanted a gentle sweet first kiss as husband and wife. And it wasn't real, it was just for show. It didn't mean anything. She could do this.

'OK,' Clover said, her voice high with anxiety. She cleared her throat. 'If I must.'

Angel laughed and she felt him relax. He turned to Brian. 'How do you want this, hands on the face, arms round the neck, what would be best photographically?'

Brian shrugged. 'I don't normally tell the bride and groom how to kiss, they choose that for themselves and I just capture it. Just go for it and if I can't get a good shot, then I'll rearrange you.'

Angel turned back to Clover and shuffled closer, his hands at her waist. She moved her hands to the lapels on his jacket and Angel bent his head down and kissed her. As soon as their mouths touched, a jolt of desire slammed into her stomach, her breath catching on her lips. He was so gentle at first, holding her like a precious treasure in his arms. She found herself sliding her hands round his neck, pressing herself up against him, and he moved his hands to cup her face. A tiny moan escaped her lips and the kiss changed to suddenly something more. He slipped his tongue inside her mouth and the taste of him sent fireworks exploding through her.

Brian cleared his throat and Clover snatched her mouth away – she'd almost forgotten he was there, every fibre of her body finely attuned to Angel.

'Sorry, um… no tongues,' Brian said, awkwardly, focussing his attention on his camera and not looking at them. 'It looks too, um… pornographic and probably not the look you were going for.'

Angel's eyes were alight with amusement as he stared down at her. 'Right, no tongues.'

'Treat her like a virgin,' Brian said and Clover snorted.

'Right, got it,' Angel said, bending his head to kiss her again.

'And don't cup her face,' Brian said. 'Your hands are too big for that.'

Angel smirked. 'I apologise for my tongue and my hands.'

'No complaints from me,' Clover said.

Angel moved both his hands to her waist and then lowered his head and kissed her again. He gave her several sweet, chaste kisses and she couldn't help giggling against his lips as Brian snapped pictures around them, taking them from different angles.

'Not like that,' Brian said, clearly getting in the swing of giving artistic direction now. 'This is your wedding day. You're about to go back to the hotel and spend the first night together as husband and wife. This kiss is the prelude to something more. We want passion, not kissing your grandma.'

Clover giggled.

'But no tongues,' Angel said.

'Right, passion but not porno.'

Angel smiled as he kissed her again, gathering her in his arms and holding her close against him. As he deepened the kiss, as the butterflies in her stomach fluttered and then took flight, she didn't think she ever wanted to stop.

'OK, I think that's enough,' Brian said. 'I have everything I need.'

Clover stepped back, eyeing Angel who was touching his lips.

'I don't think I've got everything I need,' Angel muttered darkly.

Clover cleared her throat. 'Well, thanks so much for coming Brian. Will you email me the photos when they're ready?'

He nodded.

She glanced at Angel again and then turned back to Brian. 'I'm going to get changed, so will you be able to make your way back to the hotel yourself? Take the golf buggy.'

'Great, thanks,' Brian said, shaking their hands, and then he walked off.

Clover stared at Angel as Brian got into the buggy and drove off, that kiss lying unfinished between them. Angel was breathing heavily; her heart was pounding in her chest.

Without a word, Angel stepped forward, took her face in his hands and kissed her again and this time there was no one there to interrupt them. He slid his tongue inside her mouth, tasting her, his hands caressing over her body. This was exactly what she needed to dispel the memory of Marcus once and for all.

'Let's go inside,' Angel said against her lips.

She nodded and without taking his lips from hers, he bent down and scooped her up. She let out a little shriek of laughter as he walked back towards her cottage. 'Are you carrying me over the threshold?'

'It seems fitting.'

He walked through the door and placed her down, kissing her again hard. 'God, Clover, I've wanted to do this for so long.'

She kissed him, running her fingers through his hair. He let out a little grunt of desire, the kiss getting more needful.

'We need to get out of these clothes,' Clover said and then realising as soon as she'd said it that it sounded a hell of a lot sexier than she'd intended. She just meant the dress was on hire and she needed to take it back to the shop without ruining it.

But as he kissed her his hands moved round her back and he slowly started to unzip her dress.

She felt the cold on her bare back and she froze. She stepped out of his arms and backed up against the wall behind her.

He watched her in concern. 'Are you OK?'

'Yes,' she paused. 'No. I'm sorry.'

'You don't have to apologise. I'm the one who should be sorry. I got carried away. I promised you and myself that I wasn't going to do anything you weren't ready for, but one taste of you and sense and reason went straight out the window. I'm so sorry, I thought that's what you wanted.'

'No, please don't apologise, you've done nothing wrong. I meant I needed to take the dress off before it got ruined, it's on hire. Sorry, I got scared. This is all me. I'm... broken.'

She moved away from him, a crashing feeling of disappointment slamming into her so hard it took her breath away. She tried to do her zip back up but she couldn't reach.

'Here, let me,' Angel said, gently.

She paused and he moved behind her, zipping her back into the dress.

'Thanks,' Clover muttered and then walked into the kitchen. She put the kettle on as she heard Angel move into the kitchen behind her.

She turned round to face him. It was the oddest thing to be standing there as bride and groom after what had just happened. It was safe to say the honeymoon was officially over.

'Look, I'm not going to push you on this,' Angel said. 'It's very clear we both have feelings for each other and it's also obvious that you're scared. But I don't know why. I don't think you're scared of me?'

'No, definitely not,' Clover said. Angel would never do anything to hurt her, she knew that, so why was having a relationship or being intimate with him so terrifying?

'And I think this is something more than just protecting a broken heart,' Angel said.

'Yes, it is.'

'It might be useful to tell me what this issue is. Nothing is unsurmountable and I might be able to help you with it.'

'Angel, I really bloody like you but I have a whole ton of baggage that I'm sure you don't want to deal with. In another time, another life, I think we would have been pretty spectacular together but right now...' she trailed off, shaking her head.

He moved towards her and tentatively raised a hand to stroke her cheek.

She stepped up to him and wrapped her arms around his back. He immediately enveloped her in a big hug, cradling her head.

'I'm sorry. But we'll always be friends, right?' Clover said.

He pulled back slightly to look at her. 'Always. But, as your friend, let me help you with this.'

She stared at him. 'I want that with you, I want to date and kiss and make love just like normal people do but… I don't know if I'm ready for that and honestly I don't know if I ever will be. And I'm scared you'll run away when you hear what my baggage is.'

'Not a chance, we all have baggage.'

'Some more complicated than others,' Clover said.

'It's going to have to be something really bad for me to walk away.'

'What counts as bad in your book?'

'That you secretly leave dirty socks lying around the place, that you kick puppies for fun, biting your toenails is pretty gross. Any of those are pretty bad,' Angel said.

Clover smiled. 'I promise you, it's none of those.'

'Then I think we're good.'

She took a deep breath as she studied him. She had to tell him; she knew that, even if it ruined any chance of them being together, he had to know. 'OK.'

She went and sat on the sofa and Angel came and sat next to her, looping an arm around her shoulders and pulling her into his chest.

'I don't talk about this with anyone. Aria and Skye obviously know and I think they've told Noah and Jesse some or all of it, but I don't make a habit of talking about it. So I'm just going to say this really quickly and then you can decide whether you want to stick around or not.'

Angel gave her an encouraging nod.

CHAPTER EIGHT

Clover took a deep breath. 'About three years ago, I was dating a man called Marcus who was the most disgusting, vile man I have ever met in my life. But he didn't start off that way. He was charm personified, attentive, giving me elaborate gifts. He was... lovely and everyone thought the world of him. He was one of those men that everyone loved – men, women, old people, children. He'd walk into a room and everyone would almost cheer. We'd been going out around five months when it all went wrong. One of the girls from work was having a hen night and we were going to see some male strippers. Marcus forbid me from going. I had no real interest in seeing those strippers but there was no way I was going to let him tell me what I could and couldn't do, so I went anyway.'

'Good for you.'

'Yeah, looking back now, there's a part of me that wished I hadn't, but because I did I got to see the real him and was able to get out of a toxic relationship before I got too far into it.'

'What happened? Did he hit you?'

She noticed Angel's jaw was clenched and she reached up and stroked his cheek.

'No, but in many ways what he did was worse. I went round to his house after, expecting him to be mad at me but he was really nice. Looking back now, he was way too nice. We went up to his room and started having sex and...' she closed her eyes, swallowing the bitter taste in her mouth. 'And he was filming the whole thing. After we'd finished, he showed me the video and said if I ever disobeyed him again, or if I ever left him, he would post the video on every internet site, on every form of social media that he could. My work colleagues, my friends, my family would all see me having sex.'

Angel stared at her in horror. 'Clover, that's awful.'

'I was mortified. I knew right then and there that it was over between us but there was no way I was giving him that power over me. So I apologised, even though it made me sick to do it, I told him I loved him and would never ever leave him. The next morning when he went to the gym, I took the few clothes I had at his place, stole his laptop, his camera and a memory stick I'd seen him using and I left.

'I didn't go home, I knew he'd follow me there, so I came here for a few weeks. He sent me hundreds of messages over the next few weeks, called me many times, leaving increasingly threatening voicemails, saying I had to come back or he'd share the video. I really don't think he had another copy of that video, I think I took the only copy with me or I sure as hell think it would have seen the light of day by now. It was an empty threat made to scare me. Although at the time I wasn't convinced of that but there was no way I was going back. But very quickly the threats stopped being about me coming back and started being all about the laptop, that I had to return it or he'd share the video. So I switched the laptop on and found loads of photos taken of his previous girlfriends. Most of them looked like he'd done it without their consent, when they were asleep or in the shower. There were videos too. I didn't click on those. That was why he wanted the laptop back so badly.'

'Christ.'

'And it just made me feel so sick that I had been with him all those months and had no idea what kind of hateful, repulsive man he really was. How could I not see it?'

'What happened then? I'm really hoping this story ends with Skye bumping him off and burying his body where no one would ever find it.'

Clover smiled slightly. 'Well that's when one of his exes contacted me. She'd heard through a friend of a friend we'd split up, even heard I'd taken his laptop. She told me he had ruined her life when he'd shared photos and videos of her all over the internet. She hadn't pursued it at the time with the police, it had taken all of her energy to get the videos and photos taken down from as many sites as possible, but she knew they were still out there. So together we went to the police, showed them the laptop and, to cut a long story short, he went to prison. What he did, to me and the other women, was against the law. He only got eight months which doesn't seem enough for the damage that he caused to his ex, and what he tried to do with me. But maybe he'll think twice about doing it again.'

'Well, that's good. But bloody hell, that must have hurt.'

'Oh god, it did. To know someone I trusted could betray me so viciously...' Clover shook her head. 'I think the only reason that video didn't see the light of day was because I took it with me. He destroyed his ex and was going to do the same to me.'

'I'm so sorry you went through that and it must have been

even harder if you loved him.' Angel paused. 'Did you love him?'

She hesitated because it was humiliating, even her sisters didn't know this little nugget. But Angel needed to know it all. 'He... completely swept me off my feet, I was besotted with him and I felt so lucky to be going out with him. After a few months the shine started to fade but I still thought we'd be together forever. I feel so... ashamed that I could love a man like him and so stupid that I didn't see right through him.'

'You have nothing to feel bad about, this is all him not you. And this is how emotional abusers work, they charm the birds from the trees. My sister was actually in an emotionally abusive relationship, thankfully not for long. But he was so romantic and wonderful to her in the beginning and then he started chipping away at her, told her cruel and devastating things about her body, what having sex with her was like. He systematically destroyed her over many months. He knocked her confidence so much that she was willing to do anything to please him but eventually realised it was all a power game and ended the relationship. It knocked her confidence for months after.'

'Oh no. I'm sorry she went through that. I'm lucky I didn't have that. But I guess that single act of betrayal had the same impact. I haven't had a relationship with anyone since. I've not even wanted to. The thought of sex made my stomach turn because when I think of sex, I think of him. I think about the last time we were together where he was kissing me and touching me and the whole time he was betraying me, violating me in the worst possible way, and I had no idea. I think about that video of us together that he was going to share with the world and it makes me sick. And here I am sitting next to someone wonderful, the first person I've had feelings for since that horrible excuse of a man, and I'm freaking out about the possibility of a relationship, of putting my trust in someone again. And then there's sex, the prospect of that is terrifying.'

'Of course it is, that's completely understandable. Clover, I had no idea. I knew there was some reason you were holding back, I had no idea it was as vile as that.'

They lapsed into silence for a while and Clover had no idea what he was thinking.

'It's OK if you don't want to get involved with me, I understand. It's a whole load of baggage you weren't expecting.'

'Clover, I'm not going anywhere. First and foremost, I'm your friend and I'm here for you in any way you need me. And secondly...'

He paused, smiling a little.

'Secondly?' Clover asked.

'I really bloody enjoyed that kiss and if there's a chance of doing that again at some point in the future, then I'm totally on board for that.'

She smiled, her heart filling for him.

'Are you serious? I've just told you I have all these issues and you're sticking around?'

'You don't have issues. Marcus is the one that has serious issues. What kind of scum does that? What you have are scars and they will heal because you're a brave and incredible woman. It took balls to leave him when you didn't know if there were other copies of that video, it took courage to go to the police, to stand up in court against him. I think you're amazing and I know you can do this. We can take this as slow as you want. Nothing has to change now. If you feel ready to date and go out for dinner at some point, great. If you're happy to kiss that's great too. If not, that's totally fine, we can just be friends.'

'What about sex?'

'That's a kind offer, but I'm a bit tired right now,' Angel said.

Clover laughed, actually laughed out loud, which was the first time that had ever happened while discussing this.

'I meant, how will you feel if we never have sex?'

'That will happen when you're ready and if it doesn't, it doesn't.'

'Really? You don't mind?'

'I want you to be happy, I don't want you to do something you're not comfortable with. I'd rather you felt safe and relaxed with me than stressing out about whether we're going to have sex or not.'

She smiled and leaned her head on his shoulder. 'Angel, where were you three years ago?'

'Clearly not where I was meant to be.'

They sat in silence for a while as he stroked her hair and she thought about what would have happened had she met Angel instead of Marcus.

She sat up. 'You know what, I'm not going to let that pathetic weasel of a man ruin this for us. Tomorrow night, we're going to go on a date, a proper one. And I always used to have a rule that there would be no sex until the fifth date, so that's when we're going to do it.'

He shook his head. 'There is no timetable for this, whether we make love tomorrow, Friday, six months from now or not at all, it will happen when you're ready.'

She stared at him. 'No rules.'

He shook his head. 'Not for something as important as this.'

She smiled. 'I had no idea this conversation was going to go like this. Kind of makes me wish we'd had this talk before.'

Angel shrugged. 'Maybe you weren't ready.'

She leaned her head against his shoulder again and he

kissed her forehead. For the first time in a very long time, she was now feeling positive about her future.

Clover stood at the fence at the bottom of the garden handing apple slices to Bob, Freya and Zeus, the three horses. She stroked Freya's soft nose and leaned her face against the side of her warm head.

She'd got changed out of her wedding dress and was now wearing her jeans, a long pale blue oversized hoodie and a pair of yellow wellies. It was twilight, that glorious time of day between sunset and darkness, when the rainbow-coloured autumn leaves glowed in the remains of the sunlight. The evening was cool with a promise in the air of a frost later that night.

She felt... happy and contented. She knew she had a long road ahead of her, that she couldn't just flick a switch and turn off these fears, but she had taken a huge step forward today and it had turned out so much better than she'd hoped.

For three long years she hadn't even thought about having a relationship with anyone and then Angel had come into her life and everything had changed. She'd been happy flirting with him and enjoying the chemistry that sparked between them, but most of all she had loved the wonderful friendship they had developed.

And now they were going to date. And although she knew that probably tomorrow and over the next few weeks as they took their relationship in another direction, her fear and nerves would return, right now she could only feel excitement and happiness. Part of that was taking the first steps back to normality again, to having a fun, casual relationship for the first time in three years, but a huge part of it was she was going to be doing that with Angel.

'Here you go,' Angel said as he passed her a mug of hot mulled cider.

She cupped the mug in both hands and smiled when he draped a blanket around her shoulders. He pulled a carrot from his pocket, broke it into three fairly equal pieces and offered it out to the horses. They whiffled it up.

'What were you thinking about when I came out?' Angel asked, taking a sip of his own cider. 'You looked so far away.'

'I was thinking that I'm glad it's you.'

He looked confused so she pressed on.

'Starting dating again feels like a big step and I can think of no better person to take that step with.'

He stared at her and she realised she'd made him uncomfortable. He'd opened his mouth to say something when Darcy, the cow, shoved her head over the fence to see if there was any food for her too.

Angel laughed at the intrusion as Darcy snorted over him. 'Why don't you introduce me to our neighbours?'

Clover was glad of the distraction.

'This is Darcy,' she said, handing the cow a slice of apple. 'Freya is the palomino, Bob is the piebald and the grey is Zeus.'

Angel stroked Bob's head. 'They are beautiful. When I was little I always wanted to be a farmer.'

'You did?' Clover asked. That took her completely by surprise. Angel loved to travel and staying put and spending the rest of his life tending to animals just didn't fit in with the image of the Angel she knew.

'Yeah, I had no experience or knowledge of what it meant to be a farmer but I thought they just owned lots of animals and that was enough for me. I could see myself with a few horses, a goat, some fat pigs, a few sheep. It was a very romanticised view. I don't know what I planned to do with all these animals beyond owning them or how that would make me money.'

She smiled. 'That's cute.'

'What did you want to be?' Angel asked.

'Oh, I wanted to work with animals too, but I had much grander plans than a few sheep and pigs.'

'Oh?'

'I was going to have my own zoo and it was going to be like Noah's Ark, two of every single animal in the entire world.'

'Wow, those are some grand plans. And that would have been a very big zoo too.'

'I know.'

'And where do you draw the line, do you have two dogs or two Bernese Mountain Dogs, two English Setters, two corgis?'

'I don't think I thought through the logistics or the specifics. I wasn't that keen on spiders so they were out. Camels too, after one spat at me in a zoo once. There was no room for that kind of behaviour in my zoo.'

Angel laughed and then checked his watch. 'Come on, dinner is nearly ready. And while we eat, you can tell me all about the other dreams you had as a child.'

He held out his hand and she took it. It would be lovely to think that Angel could make her dreams come true but that was too much responsibility to place on his shoulders. She had given up on so many of her dreams when Marcus had betrayed her and it was hard to even hope for those dreams now. They had to take this one step at a time and for now she was happy to focus on dating and having fun with this wonderful man.

Angel sat in his bed, listening to Clover getting ready for bed in the bathroom. He didn't know if she was going to join him again as she had the night before, but he kind of presumed and hoped she would.

It had suddenly got a lot more serious between them than he thought it would. She'd said she wasn't interested in a proper relationship, but how could it be anything but that when it would be her first relationship after what that asshole had done to her. Her trust had been betrayed in the worst possible way. No matter how casual they kept their relationship, Angel would need to give her a lot of support with that. In some ways he was honoured that she was trusting him enough to take those tentative first steps with him but he still wasn't sure if he was the right man for the job. Her comment earlier by the falls when she'd said she was glad it was him weighed heavily on his shoulders. He didn't want to let her down. He wanted to be there for her for as long as she needed, in whatever capacity she needed, but what if that was six months or more? That was certainly a hell of a lot longer than all of his other relationships. He'd never made promises about the longevity of a relationship before. All the women he'd been with had always known what they were getting from him – a few dates, a bit of a laugh, some great sex and that was it. But there was something about Clover that made him want more and he wasn't sure how to handle that.

He suddenly realised she was hovering in the doorway, watching him. He wondered how long she'd been standing there. She looked anxious.

'Is it OK if I sleep here again?'

'Of course,' Angel said, holding up the duvet for her.

She climbed into bed next to him, lying on her side as she faced him. He lay down on his side too and for a few minutes they simply stared at each other. They didn't touch, didn't say anything, and yet that spark fizzed between them, this need for more

She reached forward and stroked his face. 'You are a wonderful man Angel Mazzeo. But you don't need to worry. I'm not under any illusions what this is for you. You don't need to be scared that I'm expecting marriage and babies from this.'

'I'm not scared,' Angel said.

'I just want a few nice, normal dates with someone lovely who I know isn't going to hurt me. And then, just once, some nice, normal sex. I'm not asking for a big commitment, I know you're not looking for that.'

He stared at her, moving his hand to her shoulder and stroking down her arm. 'I can't promise forever and I can't promise nice, normal sex. In fact, I'm fairly confident that if we make love, you'll have higher praise for it than just nice.'

Clover laughed. 'You're so cocky.'

He grinned, then moved his hand to her face, stroking her cheek with his thumb. 'I think we both know where we stand with this but I can promise that I'm here for you for as long as you need me and, when it's over, we'll always be friends.'

She smiled. 'I like that.'

'Now, as your friend. How do you feel about a goodnight kiss?'

'Oh, I think that's going to be a very important part of our friendship.'

He smiled and shuffled a bit closer. As he moved his mouth to hers, he felt her breath hitch, either with nerves or excitement but it was enough for him to stall. He pulled back slightly so he could look into her eyes. 'Just a kiss, I promise.'

'I know, I trust you.'

He slowly leaned forward and captured her mouth with his. He kissed her softly and carefully at first, but when the kiss changed to something more it was she who took the lead, sliding her tongue against his, tasting him, running her hands round the back of his neck. He shifted her so she was on top, so she was in control, and she pulled back slightly to look at him. Her eyes were alight with happiness as he pushed her hair back from her face. 'I think goodnight kisses between friends arc a definite must.'

'I do too and I think if we're going to do this right, we should probably carry on for a bit longer.' She smiled and bent her head to kiss him again.

As he wrapped his arms around her and kissed her, there was a very tiny part of him that thought he could get used to this.

CHAPTER NINE

Clover was working in her office the next day, sorting out some of the wedding stuff she was going to put on the website. She only had a short while to work on it before the dance show that afternoon.

There was movement at the door and she looked up to see Aria and Skye standing there.

'Hey,' Clover said.

'We were just wondering if everything was OK, you didn't come for dinner last night,' Aria said, walking in and sitting down.

Clover blushed. She hadn't come for dinner because, after her heavy conversation with Angel, during which she'd told him everything, she'd been reluctant to leave their perfect little bubble. He'd made her dinner and they'd talked then they'd gone to bed together where they'd spent hours kissing. He'd never tried to take it any further, his hands had never wandered, he was completely respectful the whole time and she loved him a little bit because of that. Not loved him like that – she felt her mind make the quick distinction – she loved him as a friend, that was all.

'Oh my god, did something happen between you and Angel?' Skye said, reading her sister perfectly.

'I told him,' Clover said.

'And?' Aria said.

'We kissed.'

'Holy shit,' Skye said.

'Well, strictly speaking, we kissed before I told him, but after as well,' Clover said, touching her lips as she remembered the taste of him. 'And in bed with him too.'

Aria gasped. 'You slept with him?'

'No. Well only in the literal sense, not... sex.'

'This is amazing, Clover,' Skye said. 'I'm so happy for you. I know you've struggled with this for so long.'

'Well this is lovely news for a Monday morning,' Aria said. 'I've just come out of a rather dull finance meeting with Noah so I needed this. I think you just needed to find someone you trusted. I really like Angel. I think he'll be good for you.'

'I do too. We're going to try dating; we're going on a date tonight actually.'

'That's sweet, but just take things slowly,' Aria said.

'We will, we are.'

'Where are you going?' Skye asked.

'I'm not sure, I kind of just want something fun to do. It feels like we've had the big heavy conversation and, despite us both wanting something casual, it feels a lot more serious than that because of what Marcus did. I'd like to lighten the mood a little tonight.'

'Come to Cones at the Cove,' Skye said. 'You can build your own desserts, choose your own toppings and Jesse has built these great table-top marble-run games so you can play with them while you eat, plus there's giant Jenga and giant chess you can play outside if it's warm enough. It will keep you occupied so the onus isn't on romance.'

'Not a bad idea,' Clover said. 'I think the dating part I'll be able to cope with just fine. We've been friends for six months. I've spent hours talking to him, face to face and through messages while he's been away. It will just be the sex part I'll have trouble with. But he knows that and he even said if we never have sex, he'd be OK with that.'

'Wow, that's a big thing,' Skye said.

Clover couldn't help but smile at that comment from her twin. For Skye and her ex-husband, sex was such a big part of their very complicated relationship.

But Skye was right. Sex was a part of every normal relationship and it wouldn't really be fair for Angel if Clover took sex off the table completely. And there was a part of her that really wanted that with him. She wouldn't tell her sisters, but she intended to keep her fifth-date rule, if not sooner. And, as unromantic as it sounded, the sooner she could get it out of the way the better.

Clover hurried down to the village as fast as she could, hindered by her ridiculous costume. It was another freezing day but she felt very hot inside this costume. She'd managed to escape the hotel without Angel or her sisters seeing her and now she just needed to get down to the village. There was safety in numbers down there – everyone else was in costume too so she wouldn't look quite so silly. Plus all the children in the show would be dressed in the same way.

She finally reached the start of the high street and felt herself relax as Halloween hung from every area of the village green. There were zombies, witches, ghosts, cats and bats all walking around as if it was perfectly normal. Up at the far end of the village green there were a collection of kids dressed as pumpkins so she headed over to them. Some of the villagers smiled at her as she walked past and she wasn't sure if it was out of pity for what she was about to endure or amusement at her stupid, oversized pumpkin costume, green tights and green-painted face. Her blonde hair was piled inside a bright orange beret, which made the hat look like it was inflated, completing her ridiculous look.

Halfway down the high street she spotted Angel taking more photos of the fair and she sighed to herself. Of course he would be here to watch her humiliate herself.

She kept her head down hoping she could get past Angel and down to the makeshift stage without him noticing. There was lots going on in the fair, so he might not really have any interest in a kids' show.

But as if he knew she was there, his eyes suddenly found hers and his whole face lit up.

'Clover?' Angel said, moving to intercept her.

She cringed as she stopped, looking at him.

'Are you in the show?'

'Yes, I'm kind of in charge of it.'

His eyes widened. 'Why didn't you say?'

Clover gestured to her costume as if that explained everything.

'You look amazing.'

She smiled. 'You always know the right things to say, even if I don't believe you. What are you doing down here?'

'I'm here to record the show.'

Clover's heart sank. 'You're kidding? No one wants to see me and a bunch of children make tits of ourselves. That isn't going to help to sell the hotel.'

'Of course it will. This kind of thing would be gold on our

website; it says we're a child-friendly, family-friendly fun place, not just a place for retired couples to go on holiday.'

Clover sighed. 'I hate you a little bit right now.'

Angel tried to wrap his arms around her and kiss her on the nose. 'No you don't.'

'If I catch you laughing, me and you will be having words.'

He held up his hand in a Boy Scout salute. 'I promise, not so much as a smirk.'

She scowled at him and then he took her hand and walked with her through the village.

The children, all dressed as pumpkins, were waiting for them.

'Is that your boyfriend?' a feisty seven-year-old girl named Blossom asked.

Straight in with the awkward question and how was Clover supposed to answer it? She was dating Angel, although they were yet to go out on an actual date, and though there was chemistry and an obvious attraction between them, they had both agreed that it was a fun, casual arrangement. So could he really be classed as her boyfriend?

'Yes I am,' Angel replied, without any hesitation.

Clover blinked at what felt like a sudden upgrade in their relationship.

'Are you going to get married?' Darius, an eight-year-old boy, asked.

Clover looked at Angel to see how he was going to answer that one.

'We might do, one day,' Angel winked at her, clearly completely unfazed.

'My mummy and daddy just got married,' Cleo said. 'And they jump up and down on the bed. A lot.'

Blossom giggled. 'They're not jumping.'

'They are, I can hear them,' argued Cleo.

'They're having special cuddles,' Darius said, confidently.

'You can't cuddle and jump on the bed at the same time,' Cleo said.

'They lie in bed and cuddle, they don't jump on it with their feet,' Darius explained.

'They move around a lot while they have special cuddles and it sounds like they are jumping but they're not,' Blossom said.

Matilda, the youngest of the group, was watching the discussion with wide eyes, not saying anything, but Clover was sure she was taking it all in.

'My mummy and daddy were cuddling in the shower once,' Timothy said. 'They weren't lying down.'

'They were probably just having a normal cuddle, not a special one,' Blossom said.

'What are special cuddles?' Cleo asked.

'You have to jiggle about a lot,' Darius said. 'I saw Mummy jiggling in bed with Uncle Steve once. She told me not to tell anyone.'

Angel snorted next to her. Holy crap, this had just taken an unexpected turn. Thankfully there were no parents nearby as they were all waiting in their seats for the show to start. But it was time to put a stop to this before it got out of hand.

'Are we all ready for the show?' Clover asked, quickly.

The children all cheered, obviously a lot more excited about it than she was.

'Remember, it's only a bit of fun so don't worry if you go wrong,' Clover said. 'No one is going to laugh at you.'

'Good advice,' Angel said, giving Clover a pointed look.

She rolled her eyes. 'Go and find a good seat to film this, you wouldn't want to miss anything. And you need to ask the parents for permission to use the footage. If anyone has issues with it, we won't be able to use it, which would be a real shame,' she said dryly.

He grinned. 'I'm sure I can charm them into it.'

He walked off and she shook her head. She had no doubt that he would.

She quickly ran through some warm-up exercises with the kids but they were clearly itching to get on stage.

Seamus came hurrying over. 'Are we ready? Only the pig racing starts in fifteen minutes and some of the parents are eager to go and watch that.'

'Yes, we're ready to go,' Clover said, wondering if she could sneak off and watch the pig racing rather than go through with this.

She lined the children up at the edge of the stage as Seamus went out to introduce them. She heard him over the microphone.

'Ladies and gentlemen, thank you all for coming today...'

Clover peered round the curtain and saw that more of the villagers and tourists were wandering over to have a look at what was happening. Great, just what she needed.

'... We hope you are enjoying the festivities. Be sure to try the petrifying pancakes and the scary sweets. We have pig racing coming up after this in the field over there, be sure to place your bets for a chance to win some serious money. Prizes are capped at five pounds. Children are not allowed to bet but can help you to choose the winner.'

Clover smiled as Seamus rattled off the terms and conditions.

'And now I'm going to hand you over to our very own Clover Philips and the rather wonderful Pumpkin Parade.'

There was clapping and cheering from the audience as Clover and the children all walked out onto the stage, although by far the biggest cheers were coming from Angel.

She quickly lined them up, so the children were one behind the other in height order and Clover was standing at the back. The music started and as the beat kicked in the children started bouncing up and down alternately. The music changed and the children took a step to the side so half were to the right and half were to the left but Clover could see Matilda, at the front of the line, was still bouncing, unaware that she should have stepped to the right. Hoping that she would catch up, Clover carried on flapping her elbows and then touching her shoulders with opposite hands as she stepped around the stage and the children followed suit, Darius and Blossom getting it almost right, Cleo and Timothy a few seconds behind as they copied her, Matilda still bouncing at the front of the stage, clearly unaware that the dance had moved on considerably since the opening.

Suddenly Matilda peered over her shoulder and realised that she had messed up. She burst into tears, big sobbing wails that almost drowned out the music. Clover started moving over to help her, while still dancing, but now the other pumpkins had moved on to the bit where they were surrounding Clover and she couldn't get to Matilda. She glanced out into the audience and couldn't see Matilda's parents at all.

Suddenly Angel jumped up on the stage and took Matilda's hand, bringing her over to the rest of the group and dancing with her, overexaggerating all his moves which made Matilda laugh. Clover started stepping side to side, clapping her hands, and the children and Angel joined in copying her, but Darius had clearly got bored and started freestyling at the side of the stage. The audience clearly loved it and the more they laughed and clapped, the more Darius did it.

Blossom marched over and started telling him off. Cleo and Timothy had stopped to watch the drama. Angel moved over to Darius and snagged his hand, dancing back over with him to the group, much to Matilda's enjoyment, who took Darius's other hand, forming a circle. Matilda then started doing some kind of ring of roses dance, pulling Angel and Darius with her, despite Angel trying to encourage both of them to join back in.

Cleo moved over to Clover. 'I need the toilet.'

'We'll be finished in a minute,' Clover said. 'Just hold on for a bit longer.'

'I need to go now!' Cleo shouted and then ran off the stage, knocking Timothy to the floor in her haste.

Thankfully the music moved into the finale part. Darius had broken free of Angel and was now doing a robot dance, Angel and Matilda were trying to follow Clover's moves and Blossom was five steps ahead of everyone else, trying to prove that she was a good dancer while throwing evil glares at Darius. Timothy was lying on his back like a beached whale trying to get up and not quite managing it in his oversized pumpkin costume. He was giggling uncontrollably every time he failed.

Clover and Blossom struck their finale pose, Angel and Matilda copied them and Darius slid on his knees across the stage while Timothy was still rolling around on his back.

The crowd went wild, probably out of relief that the whole shambolic farce was over. Clover, Angel and the children took a bow, Darius several times, before they all shuffled off the stage.

The children ran off to find their parents as soon as they were off the stage, leaving Clover alone with Angel.

Clover stared at Angel and then burst out laughing.

'Well that was a disaster,' she said, through her laughter.

'Everyone loved it,' Angel said. 'And as you said, it was only a bit of fun.'

Seamus came off stage after announcing a few more things about the fair and moved over to shake Clover's hand.

'Absolutely marvellous Clover, well done,' Seamus said.

'Oh, I don't think it went well,' Clover said, wiping the tears from her eyes.

'I've never seen anything so funny before, and everyone enjoyed themselves, that's the important thing,' Seamus said.

He hurried off and Clover shook her head with amusement. 'They say never work with children and animals.'

'I think trained animals would have done a better job,' Angel said. He looked her up and down. 'You look bloody adorable.'

'Oh shush. But thank you for your help, I think we could make a dancer out of you.'

'I enjoyed it.'

'You should come along to one of my dance lessons.'

Angel cupped her face and kissed her nose. 'Maybe I will.'

CHAPTER TEN

Clover was just finalising the seating plan for the upcoming Christmas wedding when Delilah came rushing into her office.

'Clover, Angel has just phoned and said you need to get back to your cottage quick.'

'What? What for?'

'I don't know, he sounded pretty frantic and then he hung up before I got a chance to ask any more details.'

Clover frowned in confusion and rummaged in her bag for her mobile. She noticed four missed calls from Angel which she hadn't heard because the stupid thing had been on silent. She quickly gave him a call but it just rang and rang, without him picking up.

What could he want her for? Surely this wasn't one of his little jokes. He wouldn't have called her four times and then phoned the hotel to get hold of her if it was a joke. She hadn't seen much of him since they'd got back from the dance show earlier. He'd said he was popping back to the cottage to get the charger for his camera but that had been a while ago. What was going on?

'I'm going to have to go,' Clover said. 'If Aria is looking for me, tell her what happened.'

Delilah nodded and Clover grabbed her coat and her bag and ran outside to one of the waiting golf buggies. She jumped in and took off towards her cottage, all manner of possible scenarios running through her mind.

There was no sign of Angel round the front of the house and the cottage looked perfectly fine and not on fire or anything horrendous like that.

She spotted him near the back fence and he seemed to be struggling with something.

She quickly abandoned the buggy and ran over to him, wondering if he'd got himself stuck on the fencing somehow. Then she saw Darcy, the cow, who had stuck her head through a part of the fence that she shouldn't have been able to get her head through. Sadly this wasn't the first time.

'Oh my god, is she OK?' Clover said, hurrying to his side.

'Not really, she's got tangled up pretty bad in the wire and the more she pulls to free herself, the worse she makes it. I'm just trying to stop her pulling right now but if you can distract her with some food then maybe I might be able to untangle the wires.'

'I have wire cutters, she's done this before, though never this bad. Sing to her and I'll go and get them.'

'What?'

'She likes to be sung to, it soothes her.'

Angel stared at Clover in shock.

She suppressed a smirk at the thought of him doing that. There was no way in the world he was going to sing to a cow.

'Any particular song?' he asked.

She hesitated, unsure if he was taking this seriously. 'Well she seems to like Westlife, but anything slow should do it. I'll be right back.'

She ran inside, grabbed a handful of carrots and dug out the wire cutters from the back of a drawer then ran back out again.

She stopped in her tracks as she realised Angel was loudly singing 'What About Now' by Westlife and stroking Darcy's face. The cow had stopped struggling and was standing with half-closed eyes, enjoying the sound of Angel's deep, velvety voice washing over her. Clover couldn't help smiling as Angel reached the crescendo of the chorus. He glanced over at her and she felt her heart fill to the top for him.

She hurried over and handed him the carrots. 'Keep singing, she's loving it,' she whispered.

She crouched down and saw how badly the silly cow had tangled herself, this was going to take a lot of work. She started cutting the wire as Angel started singing 'Flying Without Wings' and feeding Darcy chunks of carrot. Slowly, Clover started untangling the wire around the cow's neck, until the point where she was finally free.

'OK, she's clear,' Clover said, standing back up. She could see Darcy was still in her element, looking totally relaxed as Angel continued to stroke her and sing to her. 'Although she looks perfectly happy to stand there a bit longer. Maybe sing a few more songs for her.'

Angel stopped singing and Darcy snapped open her eyes, seemingly glaring at him.

'Oh, she didn't like that. Quick, sing her another song,' Clover laughed.

To her surprise, he did, this time singing 'Uptown Girl'.

Clover couldn't help but laugh that Angel was still singing for the cow, and even more so when Darcy stated relaxing again.

'You're enjoying this, aren't you?' Angel muttered before launching into the chorus.

'Oh immensely.'

Although she was enjoying it not just for the comedy value, watching him show such kindness and patience to Darcy was simply wonderful to see. It filled her heart and made her feel warm inside.

Angel started singing 'Raise Me Up' and when he got to the bit about building someone up so they could stand on mountains Clover wondered if he could be the man to do that for her.

CHAPTER ELEVEN

Angel looked around Cones at the Cove with a smile. The place had changed so much since the time it had been nothing more than a shack at the bottom of the gardens of Sapphire Bay Hotel. Of course he had seen the changes when it had officially opened in the summer but he hadn't really had much cause to come down here after that, plus he'd been away a lot over recent months helping with the sale of the hotel in Dubai. He'd seen it the day before briefly when they'd had their photos taken for the wedding brochure, but the place had been closed then and, without the atmosphere of families and friends laughing over a great dessert, it hadn't shone as much as it could. But the café was thriving and he was so pleased to see it paying off.

There was a bit of a beach vibe to the place, with turquoise leather booths and driftwood-style tables. Beach balls, buckets and spades, bunting, crabbing nets and fairy lights were strewn artfully from the ceiling and the walls were beautifully painted with ice creams, sundaes and other desserts which had been done by Izzy. One wall was entirely windows, looking out over Emerald Cove. The other wall was taken up with different-flavoured soft-whip ice cream machines. These were the café's main attraction, allowing guests to build their own desserts. There was a whole buffet bar of toppings including chocolate buttons, chopped nuts, fresh fruit, coconut shavings, jelly worms, Oreos, cookies, candyfloss and so much more. There was also currently a definite Halloween theme to the flavours and toppings and added decorations around the room.

Jesse and Skye were busy making waffles, pancakes and other desserts not covered by the ones available in the main part of the café. People were sitting at tables laughing and chatting, tucking into wonderful creations. Angel noticed Sylvia at a nearby table drinking a ridiculously tall milkshake. She had a notepad and pen in front of her and he wondered if she was going to be writing down some ideas for her next story. The place looked pretty busy, a great place for people-watching.

One of the things that hadn't been there in the summer was the table-top games, the little marble-runs attached to the walls that could be built in any way the guests wanted. Jesse had made the parts and it was up to the guests to rearrange it so it worked. There was lots of laughter and good-natured groans of frustration as people tried and failed to accomplish it.

Angel turned his attention to Clover and to his surprise she was busy shredding a napkin.

'What's up?'

'Nothing,' Clover said.

He cocked his head, studying her. 'Are you nervous?'

'A little. This is the first date I've been on in over three years.'

'But it's me, we're friends, hanging out, no big deal.'

'But we're not just hanging out,' Clover said.

'What's the difference?'

'Well, if this was a real first date, I'd be trying to impress you, hoping you'd get to the end of the evening and want another date.'

'I'm already impressed and, I promise, this will be the first date of many.'

She smiled, relaxing a little.

'And this *is* a real date,' Angel said. 'I'm not going out with you as a favour to you or because I feel sorry for you. I'm a nice guy but I'm not that altruistic. I enjoy spending time with you, holding your hand, kissing you, laughing with you. And if or when you're ready to take this further, well I'll enjoy that very much too. Believe me, I want to be here as much as you do. Or maybe more than you currently.'

She laughed. 'I want to be here too.'

'Then relax.'

'Do you not think we should be asking date questions like, what's your best quality, or what's your biggest weakness?'

'Are you interviewing me for a job?'

She laughed. 'Sorry, is that too serious? How about favourite colour or animal?'

'I'm not sure that would reveal any more about my character. OK, how about, if you won a million pounds right now, what would you spend it on?'

'Ooh, that's a good one. Although, I'm very happy with my life right now so I'm not sure what I'd spend my money on. I love being here on Jewel Island. The hotel has always been my home, me and Skye were even born here, up in my parents' old apartment where Aria and Noah now live. And I know I left because I was young and wanted to see a bit of the world beyond the hotel walls but when this thing with Marcus happened, this place was my haven, and when Dad got sick and died, I knew I wanted to stay here and help to keep the place going. Now I get to work alongside my sisters every day and I love it. I love teaching dance too, it's all I've wanted to do.'

'Apart from run your own zoo,' Angel said.

Clover laughed. 'Yeah, impossible childhood dreams don't count.'

'Sure they do.'

'Well I wanted to dance when I was a kid too. I used to dance everywhere, down in the village, at school, I couldn't stop.'

'OK, I'll let you have that. So are you saying you don't want my hypothetical million pounds I'm offering you?' Angel asked.

'I'm not saying I don't want it, just that I'd struggle to know what to do with it. The cottage belongs to the hotel so I have no mortgage or anything to pay off. I'd probably go on holiday, buy some food and things for the horses, I always feel I'm short of that. I'd give some to my sisters and probably give the rest to charity.'

He smiled. He loved her generosity.

'Which charities would you bestow your fortune on?'

'Oh well, I lost both my parents to cancer so probably some of it would go to cancer charities and then probably some animal charities too. I'm a sucker for an animal in need.'

He smiled. Of course she was. Watching her with Darcy today had been completely infectious. He loved animals but he'd never thought he would find himself singing to a cow to calm her down. But somehow that kind of thing made sense when he was with Clover.

'What would you do with it?' Clover asked.

'Well charity obviously—'

'Which charity?'

'Alzheimer's Society,' Angel said without missing a beat and he saw her cock her head as if she was about to ask him why. He decided to move on. He didn't really want to get into that on their first date. 'And then I'd probably just use the rest to travel more, to the places I want to see rather than the places I have to travel to for work.'

'You wouldn't buy a house, settle down?'

'I'm not ready for that yet.'

She watched him for a moment as if he was a puzzle she was trying to solve.

'OK, I have a question,' Clover said and he braced himself for something serious. 'If you could choose a superpower, which one would it be?'

He laughed. 'Wow, pulling out the big guns now with those kinds of questions.'

'Well, I'm taking this dating malarkey very seriously.'

Suddenly Skye arrived at the table. 'Can I get you any drinks while you decide what you want? I can recommend the milkshakes or the hot chocolates, we have lots of flavours for both.'

'What flavour milkshakes do you have?' Angel asked.

Skye rattled off a list a mile long including some flavours it had never occurred to Angel could work as a milkshake.

'I'll have the pecan pie flavour please,' Clover said.

'I'll try the maple syrup and chocolate flavour,' Angel said.

'Coming right up,' Skye said, before heading back towards the kitchen.

'I can see your sister is in her element here,' Angel said.

'Oh, she loves doing stuff like this. Noah made all her dreams come true.' Clover eyed Jesse who was delivering a big sundae to one of the other tables. 'Well, not *all* of them.'

Angel decided to get the date back on track. 'So, superpowers. That's a hard one, there are so many good ones. But I think I would go for something like precognition.'

'Seeing into the future? Doesn't that spoil the fun if you know how life is going to work out? That's like reading the end of the book before you read the rest.'

'True, but wouldn't it be nice to see the consequences of your decisions before you made them? Maybe change your mind if necessary.'

'I don't know, some of the best things that happen in life are unexpected, serendipitous. We can't plan for everything and sometimes it's better when we don't,' Clover said.

'Maybe. I'd kind of like to look back on my life with no regrets. Maybe the gift of foresight could help with that.'

Clover clearly thought about this for a moment. 'Well the gift of foresight would certainly have stopped me from going out with Marcus.'

'Exactly. What would be your superpower?'

'I'd be a shapeshifter.'

Angel smiled. 'That's cool. Most shapeshifters, especially in fiction, have the ability to change into just one animal so which—'

'Oh no, I'd have the ability to change into anything I wanted, cow, dragon, a sofa.'

Angel burst out laughing. 'A sofa? What need would you have to turn into a sofa?'

'You never know when the occasion would arise, but if it did, I'd be ready.'

He shook his head in amusement. He really liked Clover, she made him smile so much.

He reached across the table to take her hand but, before he could, he was interrupted by Jesse placing their milkshakes in the middle of the table.

'Has Skye got you working here on your holiday?' Clover asked.

'Ah, I might as well make myself useful,' Jesse said. 'Besides, as long as I'm with her I don't mind.'

Clover smiled and shook her head. 'You two have the strangest relationship.'

Jesse cleared his throat, seemingly keen to change the subject. 'Have you decided what you would like? We have several Halloween specials, or would you prefer to build your own desserts?' he asked, opening up his notepad.

'Oh, I think I'll build my own,' Clover said.

'Me too,' Angel said.

'Good choice, I'll be right back with your bowls.' Jesse left them alone.

Angel turned his attention back to Clover. 'So, shapeshifting...'

'Yes, are you jealous of my superpower?' Clover said.

'I am a bit. I think you picked a good one there, my super-power is a bit dull in comparison.'

'I'll let you change your mind if you want.'

'Hmm, OK then, telekinesis,' Angel said.

'Now that would be cool.'

'Yeah, I could get every flavour ice cream in this place with every topping without getting up from the table.'

'Telekinesis. The power of laziness.'

Angel laughed.

Jesse returned with the bowls and spoons and then a few seconds later came back with some napkins. Angel watched him join Skye near the kitchen and they exchanged words as they looked over in their direction. He wondered if they were trying to chaperone them again. Although Clover didn't seem any the wiser.

'This is a great place for a date, it's fun,' Angel said, testing the waters. 'It was a good suggestion to come here.'

'Oh, it was Skye's idea,' Clover said.

Angel smirked. Of course it was. At least Clover hadn't deliberately chosen this place so her twin could look after her; Clover just wanted to support her sister.

'Why don't we go and get our desserts,' he said.

'How about we build a dessert for each other?'

'I like that idea.'

'It's a lot of pressure though,' Clover said. 'You don't want to ruin my date by giving me a dodgy dessert.'

'No, I definitely don't want that.'

'This could be the make or break of us,' Clover said.

'Wow, that is a lot of pressure.'

'Are you up for it?'

'Of course. I won't let you down.'

Clover grinned. 'It would be quite hard to do that actually. Skye's ice creams are amazing and I think I would be happy with any flavour.'

'Yes but the right combination of toppings is important too.'

'OK, let's do this.'

Clover stood up and Angel was surprised to see that she was going to the toppings bar first. She clearly had a tactic. He moved over to the wall of ice creams and studied the flavours. There were so many to choose from and although Clover wasn't taking this remotely seriously, he wanted to get this right.

Suddenly he spotted the Toblerone flavour, which she had mentioned she wanted to try a few days before in a pancake. They'd had a pancake at the fair but the stand hadn't had any Toblerone left so Clover had settled for Nutella instead. He served himself a good dollop of the Toblerone and then looked around for the salted caramel too as that had been the other flavour she'd mentioned and hadn't been able to try. He found that and added a large blob to the bowl. OK, a third flavour. What would complement the flavours he'd already chosen? His eyes fell on coconut. He'd had a coconut Toblerone once and it had been lovely. He quickly added a squirt of that to the bowl and then moved over to the toppings as Clover moved past him with a wink and a smile which made him feel warm inside.

He didn't want to overkill the dessert and put a ton of toppings on it, so he decided he would just stick to three like the ice creams. Cashew nuts, he'd seen several packets of those in her kitchen cupboards. He grabbed a scoopful of them and sprinkled them over the top. He grabbed a scoop of fresh strawberries next as that and chocolate was always a great combination. Lastly he grabbed some jelly worms, just because it was fun and this date was supposed to be about that, after all.

He returned to their booth and watched Clover as she finished up with the ice creams and then moved back over to the toppings again. There was something about her that he found so compelling. She was beautiful, there was no denying that, but his attraction to her felt so much deeper than that. He couldn't take his eyes off her. He watched her as she carefully selected the toppings, thinking about some of them very carefully, and as she added some she had a big smile on her face. She was utterly captivating.

Clover came back to the table with a mischievous smile on her face. She had a silly sense of humour and he loved that.

She sat down but before she could speak he leaned over, cupped her face and kissed her. Her lips against his was the most incredible feeling in the world. What was it about this woman that made him want to kiss her all the time, and why did it feel so damned good? Maybe just because they were friends. He'd never really had any female friends before so this was all new for him but if this was what it felt like to date a friend, he definitely wanted to do more of that in the future.

She smiled as he sat back down, her whole face lighting up. 'You know, you're pretty good at this dating game malarkey. The women you date must love you if this is how you treat them.'

He sat back in his seat and took a sip of his milkshake as he thought. He suddenly felt bad for all the women he'd been with before. He had never treated them badly but he certainly hadn't gone out of his way to make them feel special. But his history with women had never been anything serious and they'd known that. This thing with Clover felt different. Not serious because they'd both agreed they didn't want that, but different.

'I'm not kissing you to score points with you or doing any of this to make you smile, although when I do make you smile it does make me feel warm inside. I'm kissing you because I want to, because being with you makes me happy. There is no game here.'

She stared at him in surprise and then cleared her throat. 'Well, shall we swap desserts. What did you do for me?'

'Toblerone and salted caramel ice cream because you wanted that at the fair the other day, and coconut as the wild card, because I think coconut goes with most things. For the toppings, cashew nuts because I know you love them, strawberries because they go well with chocolate, and jelly worms because, well, it is Halloween.'

She smiled as she took the dessert from him. 'Wow, you do pay attention.'

'When it matters.'

She took a few spoonfuls and he watched her, transfixed.

'Mmm, this is amazing, you've chosen the perfect combination. Thank you.'

He smiled. 'What did you get for me?'

'Well, I think you should try to guess,' Clover said, sliding the bowl across the table towards him.

There were three distinct-coloured ice creams. He took a small spoonful of one and smiled. 'Orange.'

'Yes, because I noticed my satsumas have taken a bit of a dent since you moved in.'

He grinned and took a spoonful of the yellow one. 'Oooh, is that mango?'

'Yes it is. Because I know you like to travel and thought you needed something exotic while you're here in dreary old England.'

'It's not been dreary since I've been back.'

'I know, we've been really lucky with the weather for the fair.'

'I wasn't talking about the weather.'

She smiled and focussed her attention on her dessert for a moment as he tucked into his last flavour of ice cream. It was white and there were bits in it, so for a moment he thought it was coconut too, but when he tasted it he realised what it was. 'White chocolate.'

'Well, I love white chocolate so I figured if you didn't, I could have some of it too.'

He laughed. 'Good call, but sadly I love white chocolate, it's my favourite thing. But as I'd like to be a gentleman on our date, I'm happy to let you have some.'

He scooped up a big dollop and held it across the table for her. She leaned forward and with her eyes locked on his she sucked the ice cream from his spoon.

Christ, the intimacy of that simple act was not something he'd been expecting. Neither had he been expecting the punch of desire to his stomach. He saw Clover's eyes darken as she stared at him, obviously she was thinking the same too.

When she'd finished he dipped his spoon back into his dessert, trying to cool his thoughts and steer them away from dragging Clover back to her house and making love to her in front of the fire. He'd told her he was happy to wait until she was ready and he was never going to do anything to pressure her into it, but Christ that didn't stop him from thinking about it. He licked the spoon of white chocolate himself and he felt another kick to the stomach as he could still taste her.

He rooted around to find the toppings at the bottom that Clover had hidden; he needed something, anything else to focus on right now. There were chopped nuts and chocolate buttons on the top but he knew there was something under-neath too. He smiled as he saw spiders, eyeballs and jelly fingers all covered by the ice cream. Clover giggled as she realised he'd found them. There was no explanation needed for any of those toppings, she'd done it simply to make him laugh and he liked that.

Dating Clover was going to be a whole lot of fun.

Clover stared at the flames of the fire as they crackled and danced in the fireplace. Tonight had been lovely. They'd talked and laughed and played games and now they were back in her cottage, the fire burning away, Angel making them hot choco-late in the kitchen. It felt so domesticated and cosy and real. He was very easy to get on with and so bloody lovely. She'd known this of course, as soon as they'd met they'd hit it off straightaway, so it was no great surprise that they were getting on so well, but now they were dating it just seemed so much more significant. This kind of connection was what she'd always wanted. When she'd imagined her forever, it was this. But this thing with Angel was never going to be that, they both knew it. At least she now had a standard to compare her future relationships with, a baseline. It had to be this good or there was no point in continuing with it. She wouldn't settle for anything less.

Angel came in and placed the two mugs on the table in front of her before sitting down and slinging his arm round her shoulders. She leaned into him, resting a hand on his chest, feeling his heart beating steadily against her fingers. She looked up at him and he simply stared back, a smile on his face, his eyes locked on hers. They didn't say anything, there was no need for that. Butterflies fluttered in her stomach and she leaned up and kissed him, briefly.

All she needed to do was find a man exactly like Angel. Surely that wasn't going to be that hard? She ignored the doubt in her mind that said that no man would ever come close to being as good as Angel.

CHAPTER TWELVE

Clover moved around her dance studio chatting to her class of ballet beginners the next morning. Because she was teaching a lot of the hotel guests who were only there for a week or so, most of her classes never really went beyond the beginner stage. The islanders came and went whenever they had the time, but not many of them turned up on a weekly or daily basis so she just kept things light and easy. As long as people moved and had fun, she was happy. Sylvia O'Hare, who was well into her eighties, was one of the guests who had attended that day, and most of Clover's participants were elderly, although she did run a few children's classes too.

'Hello Sylvia, lovely to see you here,' Clover said.

'Well, I can't just stay in my room writing my stories all day, I need to stretch the old bones.'

'That's definitely a good idea. Have you done much dancing before?'

'I was a wonderful dancer back in the day,' Sylvia said, modestly. 'But mostly ballroom dancing – tango, salsa, that kind of thing.'

'Well this is a little different to that. For one there'll be no partner, not in the beginning lessons.'

'Do you have hunky men come in for the advanced lessons? Because I'd definitely be interested in that, especially if they're wearing those figure-hugging tights.'

Clover laughed. 'Sadly not. Generally we would partner with each other, but as I said that comes later, we have to get the basic moves down first.'

Sylvia sighed theatrically as if she was being deprived.

'I'm sure you'll cope without the hunky men.'

Clover looked at the clock and realised it was time to start. She moved to the front, pressed play on the music and turned it down low, so it was more background noise.

Just as she was about to start, the door to the studio was pushed open and Angel poked his head round.

'Hey,' he said.

Clover couldn't help the smile from filling her face, something Sylvia picked up on straightaway.

'Hi,' Clover said.

'Did I miss the class?'

'No, we're just about to start.' Clover cocked her head in confusion. 'Did you want to join?'

Angel pushed the door open and stepped inside and Clover burst out laughing when she realised he was wearing a pair of bright blue tights that showed every single lump and bump. He'd teamed it with a t-shirt that had a hippo wearing a tutu.

'You most certainly can,' Sylvia said, her eyes wide like a kid on Christmas morning. She hurried over and linked arms with Angel, bringing him further into the room. 'You can be my partner.'

Clover smirked. Angel had the silliest sense of humour and she loved he had turned up today like this, presumably just to put a smile on her face.

'You look... lovely,' Clover said.

'Well, I wanted to do it properly.' Angel's eyes cast down to the leggings she was wearing and the long t-shirt that covered her bum and shook his head in disapproval. 'I was kind of hoping I'd see you in a fetching leotard, leg warmers and a frilly tutu.'

'Maybe you two should save the dressing up for behind closed doors,' Sylvia said.

Clover couldn't keep her eyes away from Angel's significant bulge and neither, it seemed, could any of the other elderly guests who were giggling between themselves.

Sylvia moved behind Angel to openly admire his bum and gave Clover a theatrical wink and a thumbs up of approval.

Clover blushed and laughed.

Angel turned round to see what Sylvia was doing and she tried and failed to look innocent. He shook his head in amusement.

'OK, let's get started,' Clover said.

Angel straightened his face, giving Clover his full attention. How was she supposed to concentrate when he was looking at her like that?

'We're going to start off with a few warm-up exercises, so turn your head to the side and the other side...'

She took them through various gentle stretches, tailoring the exercises for some of the older participants.

'Now this warm-up is called reverence. You're going to point your toes and take a step to the side like this, just tap your toe on the floor before you put your foot down. Now both feet together and bend your knees. That's it and now repeat to the other side.'

She suppressed a smile as Angel wobbled, standing on one leg, but he was doing a good job pointing his toes.

The other ladies were following dutifully.

'The next one is called reveré and we're simply going to bend our knees and then go up on our tiptoes and repeat.'

She moved around the class, gently correcting postures as she went. When she reached Angel she placed a gentle hand on his back, to move him into the right position. Even his back was solid muscle. He glanced at her and the look he gave her sent goosebumps across her skin. They hadn't touched much, beyond some lovely hugs and kisses. Maybe that was something that could change tonight, build up to the big event slowly. The way he was looking at her suggested he wanted that too.

She lingered with her hand on him for a moment or two longer than necessary and it was only when she noticed Sylvia watching them with a smirk on her face that Clover moved away and went back to the front.

Clover cleared her throat. 'The next one is an exercise for our arms, it's called port de bras. You're going to put your arms in front of you as if you're hugging a huge ball, elbows up and out and hands down so they're level with your belly button. Middle fingers almost touching, and trying to be as fluid and graceful as you can, raise your hands above your head but keep the same shape, don't drop that ball. Then bring your arms down to shoulder height. And back to the front.'

Clover watched her class carefully, trying not to make eye contact with Angel as she repeated the first part of the exercise again, raising her arms in the air. 'Now we're going to bend at the waist so our bodies are at a complete right angle.'

'Your body might be,' Sylvia grumbled. 'I don't think I'll ever be able to stand back up if I bend that far down.'

Clover grinned. 'Or bend as far as you're comfortable with and, if you can, bend down and touch the floor, but only if you're happy with that.'

Angel, unsurprisingly, could touch the floor with ease and Clover distinctly heard Sylvia mutter that he was a show-off.

Clover talked them through the five basic positions which involved having the feet out to the side with their feet at different angles.

'OK, now we are going to use some props,' Clover said, picking up her box and handing out short chiffon scarves. It was surprising how easy it was to be graceful with a chiffon scarf. The material was so light, it practically floated with only the slightest movement. Using a scarf naturally encouraged lighter, more gentle movements because you could see the reflection of your moves in it.

Clover moved around the class encouraging them to do a ballet walk, or the tendu, which was touching the floor with their tiptoes then the balls of their feet, and waving their arms in the air in slow, careful fluid motions. Everyone seemed to be enjoying themselves. One member perhaps a bit too much.

Angel was punctuating his movements with pirouettes which were pretty graceful considering his size, and some pretty impressive attempts at an arabesque, with one leg off the floor, a lovely chaîné, which was a spin, and even a very spectacular saut de chat, which was the big leap that was often used as the grand finale in a dance, although he definitely needed work on his landing. He was doing all this and still waving his scarf around in an elegant fashion.

The old ladies were laughing so much they could barely concentrate on their own moves, and while Angel being over the top with his dancing was definitely cause for a laugh, Clover guessed that something else was causing the giggles. Because every time Angel jumped or spun around, certain bulges in his tights were jiggling and wobbling around as if they had a mind of their own. He would certainly benefit from a dance belt or some kind of cup if he was going to take up ballet on a regular basis. She wondered if he had any idea what was causing the laughter, or whether he simply didn't care.

Eventually, after a few more examples of some more basic moves, the lesson came to an end.

The old ladies thanked her and then thanked Angel too, as they left, still chuckling.

Sylvia gave him a big hug. 'Best laugh I've had in a long time.'

'Oh glad to oblige,' Angel said.

'I might have to write my next book about a hunky ballet dancer,' Sylvia said.

'Well, I'm happy to be your muse.'

Sylvia left them alone, chortling to herself.

Clover shook her head with a smile.

Angel brushed his hand through his hair. 'I'm sorry if I disrupted your lesson.'

She moved over to him and looped the scarf she was carrying round his neck, tugging him towards her. 'You great big silly man, I adore you and your ridiculous sense of humour. The whole point of these lessons is for people to have fun and we definitely ticked that box today. Although I'm not sure if it was your dancing or something else that tickled their fancy.'

He snaked his hands around her back and stared at her with wide innocent eyes and a smirk playing on his lips. 'What do you mean?'

'I think you know exactly what I mean,' Clover said, leaning up and kissing him. He held her tighter in his arms, kissing her as he smiled against her lips. She slid her hand down his back and gave his bum a playful squeeze. 'Where did you get these tights from anyway?'

'You can get anything from Amazon. I ordered them yesterday.'

She shook her head and kissed him again.

Just then the door to the studio opened and Clover leapt back away from him, thinking it might be a guest, but realised it was Noah.

'Oh sorry, didn't mean to interrupt anything.' Noah looked away awkwardly and then back again as he took in what Angel was wearing. He stared at Angel with a mixture of shock and confusion. 'I don't think I even want to know what's been going on here.'

'A ballet lesson,' Angel said, unashamedly.

Clover smirked. She got the distinct impression that Angel loved to wind Noah up with his ridiculous t-shirts, and the tights were a whole new level.

'Well, I was going to suggest we all had lunch together but maybe you might want to get changed first. Don't want to frighten the guests.'

'I think some of them might like it,' Angel said, not taking it remotely seriously.

'I think some of them might be put off eating their lunch if they see that.'

'I think somebody might be jealous,' Angel muttered loud enough for Noah to hear.

Noah burst out laughing. 'Come and join us when you're ready, both of you.'

With that he left the room.

Clover laughed, pulling Angel back in for another kiss. 'You walk a fine line with him.'

'He loves me really.'

Clover smiled. 'I'm sure he does.'

~

The restaurant of the Sapphire Bay Hotel had a wall of windows that overlooked Pearl Beach. Clover could see children playing on the beach, building sandcastles and splashing in the waves, despite the cooler weather.

It was past two o'clock so there were only a few stragglers left in the restaurant for lunch enjoying the views and the wonderful food. They always had a progress meeting over lunch every Tuesday to keep up to date with what was going on, sometimes at other times in the week too but Tuesday was kind of set in stone.

Clover took another bite of her burger, which was delicious. She glanced over at Angel who had at least got changed, although it seemed Noah still hadn't got over it – he was busy telling Aria, Skye and Jesse how traumatised he was from seeing his assistant in tights.

'I think some of the ladies in the class enjoyed having a male member today,' Clover said, loyally.

Angel snorted and Clover blushed at the unintentional double entendre.

'I bet they did,' Skye said, shaking her head with laughter.

Noah rolled his eyes in mock despair, muttering something about standards. He finished off his salad and pushed the plate to one side, bringing out a notebook and pen. 'How are we finding this week, is the Halloween festival proving a success?'

Clover exchanged a smile with Aria. Noah was a lot more relaxed now than he had been when he'd first come to the hotel, but he still took the running of the hotel seriously.

'It's been a huge success,' Aria said. 'We're completely sold out for the entire week, and that's the first time that's happened since the grand reopening of the hotel in the summer. I know we are sold out most weekends, but to be sold out for an entire week is a big achievement. The guests have all been full of how brilliant the festival is in the village and I know the villagers have enjoyed having it here too. It feels like the island has come alive again.'

Noah nodded. 'From my point of view this couldn't have gone any better. And we have the big ball on Halloween to mark the end of the festival, I think everyone is looking forward to that. Oh and on that note, the firework display team will be here in the next few days to set everything up for the ball, just in case you see any of them wandering round the grounds. Skye, how is everything going down at Cones at the Cove? Are you getting enough custom?'

Clover knew that when her sister had officially opened the ice cream café in the summer she'd had a bit of trouble getting people through the doors. The café was tucked away at the very bottom of the gardens and people simply didn't know it was there. Although she was quite sure that hadn't been the case recently.

'Yes,' Skye answered. 'Since Angel did that video trailer for us which plays in the hotel reception, the number of customers has gone through the roof. And the brochure for the festival you're giving out to all the guests this week has helped, plus all the Halloween-themed desserts we're doing have been very popular. Poor Jesse has been rushed off his feet,' she smirked at her ex-husband.

Clover smiled. It was clear that Jesse didn't mind working through his holiday. As long as he was with Skye, that was all that mattered.

'Skye has decorated the whole café,' Jesse said. 'It looks spectacular down there and very spooky. The kids love it.'

'Yes, I saw that when we were there for the wedding shoot and last night,' Angel said. 'It looks great. I'll pop down today or tomorrow and take some photos of the decorations and themed desserts so we can update the website with all the Halloween stuff.'

'Yes Clover, I meant to ask you about that,' Noah said. 'How did the wedding photo shoot go?'

Clover cleared her throat, suddenly finding herself blushing again. She glanced at Angel who was smiling.

'Very well,' Clover said. 'The photographer took hundreds of photos; I think we're going to get some great shots for the wedding brochure. I should get them in a few days and then we can go through them together.'

After she had carefully removed any photos of her and Angel's porno kiss.

'Great,' Noah said. 'Actually you can liaise with Angel on that, he can help to design the brochure.'

Angel grinned at her. 'Fine by me.'

'And how are we doing for staff?' Noah moved on, clearly not noticing the unspoken looks between her and Angel. 'I know that Tilly and Delilah are both working full time now that Tilly has returned from her maternity leave. Plus there's Xena but maybe we need a few more receptionists. What about in other parts of the hotel? As things get busier, we'll need more staff.'

'I could do with a few more part-time hands in Cones at the Cove,' Skye said. 'A few waiters or waitresses or people to help in the kitchen.'

'OK,' Noah said, making some notes.

'I think we could do with a few more cleaners and house-keepers to service the bedrooms,' Aria said. 'Now we're having a much larger volume of customers through the doors, we need more staff to clean up after them.'

'Right, OK. I'll do some adverts.'

'It'd be great if we could advertise locally first, I'm sure there might be some islanders who would be grateful for the work,' Aria said, loyally.

'Of course,' Noah said. 'We can always widen the net if we don't get any takers. I think it's important to get a full quota of staff especially for the coming months. I've got some ideas about how we can attract more visitors on a regular basis. Angel's Facebook ads are doing great to capture people's attention but I still feel we can do more. I think we can do more events like this, maybe one a month, something that the whole village can get involved in.'

Aria grinned. 'While I think that's a great idea, this took a hell of a lot of planning and organisation to pull off. I'm all for some events we can stagger throughout the year but one a month might be a bit too ambitious.'

Noah nodded to concede this.

Aria stroked his shoulder to soften the blow. 'Noah has just sold the majority of his shares in his New York and London hotels, which means he's stuck here forever now.'

'I'm not *stuck* here. I did that because I want to be here with you and not have to keep jetting off around the world to sort out problems in my other hotels all the time,' Noah said, defensively. 'This is my home now, and I want to stay here.'

'And I'm glad to have you here, but I do wonder if you might get bored of this quiet life, hence the need to organise all these events,' Aria said.

Noah stared at her as if no one else was at the table with them. 'I could never get bored of being with you.'

Aria smiled and leaned her head against his shoulder. He placed a kiss on her forehead.

'But you're probably right, organising an event every month might be pushing it a bit,' Noah said.

'So that's it, no more business trips?' Clover said.

'No. I'm never leaving here again. Well, apart from any holidays.'

Clover glanced over to look at Angel to see how he would react to that, knowing how much he enjoyed the travelling part of his job. He was focussed on finishing the last of his lunch but there was the tiniest hint of a frown on his forehead.

It didn't seem he was entirely happy about that. They were going to a restaurant that night for their second date. She would have to talk to him about all this then to see how he really felt.

CHAPTER THIRTEEN

Angel was waiting for Clover in the lounge of her cottage as she got ready upstairs for their date. He didn't really care what she wore to their date but as she appeared to be making an effort, he'd decided to do the same and had put on trousers and a shirt. He knew she needed this, that she wanted some kind of normal relationship, even if it was only going to last a few weeks or months. He didn't mind, he got to spend more time alone with Clover, getting to know her better, and as it was a date, he was pretty much guaranteed there'd be more kissing.

While he was waiting he flipped through some photos on his phone, looking at pictures of his travels. He'd done a lot in his life, seen so much. But he still felt there was so much out there to see and experience.

He heard Clover coming down the stairs and he looked up.

She was wearing a short blue dress that finished just above the knee in a little frill that sashayed as she moved. There were tiny butterflies embroidered around the bottom, taking flight towards the top of the dress in a range of bright colours.

Her hair tumbled down over one shoulder in lazy golden curls. Her eyes were alight with happiness and he noticed she was wearing some kind of sparkly eyeshadow that made her look magical. She looked utterly lovely.

'Clover, you look beautiful,' Angel said.

She batted him away affectionately. 'You know all the right things to say.'

He caught her by the waist. 'It's true.'

She smiled and leaned up and kissed him. Her kiss was so addictive, as soon as their lips touched it was like a high that no drug could recreate. He wrapped his arms around her, holding her close against him.

He pulled back slightly. 'Let's forget the date and just stay here and do this all night.'

'Tempting. But I really fancy a steak.'

'More than you fancy me?' Angel said.

Clover wrinkled her nose which made him smile. 'I'd say it's about even right now. You have the whole night to try to inch ahead. But Gabriel's steaks are amazing, so you have pretty tough competition.'

She pulled out of his arms and went to get her coat as if the kiss hadn't affected her at all.

He took her coat from her and she looked at him in confusion, until he offered it out to her, holding it open so she could put it on.

'Oh, very gentlemanly.'

'Well, if we're on a date, we need to do things properly.'

'So you're not trying to score brownie points?' Clover said, turning her back to him and shrugging into her coat.

'Oh, I'm definitely trying to score brownie points. For the sake of my own pride I'd like to score higher than a piece of steak tonight.'

Clover smiled and then grabbed his coat and held it out for him.

He burst out laughing and then let her help him into his coat.

'I believe in equal opportunities,' Clover said.

'So do I, but if I'm going to win against a piece of meat tonight, I'm going to pay for tonight's dinner.'

He expected her to protest against it, but she simply nodded. 'That's fine.' She opened the front door, wrapping a scarf around her neck as she stepped outside into the twilight. 'As long as I can pay for the next date.'

He smiled and stepped outside with her. The sky had that scarlet glow at the horizon. The sun had already set but its rays were still splayed across the inky sky. It made the autumn leaves glow that more dramatically.

He held out his arm for her and she smiled and slid her hand into his elbow.

'Are you this old-fashioned with all the women you date?' Clover said as they followed the path from her cottage towards the twinkling lights of the village.

'Old-fashioned?' Angel protested, suppressing a smirk. 'Are you criticising my moves?'

'Nooo, never,' Clover feigned innocence. 'I just figured that Angel Mazzeo was a bit more of a Casanova than this. I thought you'd be the kind of man that kisses a woman and unhooks her bra at the same time.'

Angel laughed loudly. 'I don't know whether to be offended or flattered by that.'

'Don't be offended, you're being really sweet and I appreciate it. I just wasn't really expecting it.'

They walked on in silence for a few moments. But Clover was right, all this was different for him.

'I don't normally date,' Angel said. 'Not really.'

'What does that mean?' Clover looked up at him, the moonlight catching the sparkles on her eyes. With a million stars shining brightly behind her, she looked... enchanting and he just wanted to kiss her again, so he did. He pulled her to a stop and cupped her face in his hands and kissed her. Up there on the hill surrounded by the muted darkness, it felt like they were the only two people in the world.

For reasons he couldn't quite understand, he felt like he wanted to capture this moment, just like thousands of other beautiful sights he'd taken photos of before. He wanted to remember this.

He pulled back slightly to look at her.

'What was that for?' she said, her voice coarse.

'Just because I wanted to. Is it OK if we take a photo?'

'Oh, OK.'

He quickly fished his phone out of his pocket, ignoring the look of confusion on Clover's face. He looped an arm round her shoulders and positioned the phone to get the stars and the moon in the sky behind them and the twinkling lights of the village. Clover was still looking a bit bemused by the whole thing, so he set the phone to capture multiple shots and then kissed her on the cheek while the phone did its thing. She smiled and turned to face him, kissing him on the mouth. He found himself smiling when she slid her tongue into his mouth.

She pulled back with a mischievous grin on her face. 'I thought if you were going to take a photo, we might as well do one with porno tongue as Brian isn't here to stop us.'

Angel laughed as he glanced at his phone to see what the photos were like. The first one was of her smiling, her eyes closed as he kissed her cheek, and it made a lump of emotion catch in his throat. The next was of them about to kiss properly and they both looked so happy. The next few were of them kissing and it was so passionate, so intense, it looked like they were about to rip each other's clothes off right then and there.

'Happy?' Clover asked.

He cleared his throat and shoved his phone back in his pocket. 'Yes. They're fine. Let's go.'

He took her hand and they walked down towards the village.

~

Clover's favourite restaurant was a simple affair. It was a white room with black and white photos of impressive buildings and bridges. There were black leather booths around the room, and wooden reclaimed floorboards that looked like they had been around hundreds of years. Although the décor was fairly basic, the food was incredible, the flavours of something as simple as steak so intense, just the thought of it made her mouth water.

'What did you mean before when you said you don't date?' Clover said. They'd placed their order and were snacking on nachos as they waited for it to come.

Angel smirked. 'You don't miss anything, do you? I'm sure this is not going to put me in a good light but the women I've been with over the last few years have all been casual. We might go out for a drink but generally it just involves sex.'

Clover picked up a nacho and broke a chunk off. 'So you don't spend time talking or having fun with these women?'

He grinned. 'We have plenty of fun.'

Clover laughed. 'I mean, being silly, apple bobbing, going to a fair, chatting for no other reason than just to get to know one another.'

'No, there's not really much of that.'

'Then why are you doing that stuff with me?'

'Because you're my friend.'

'Do you not have any other female friends?'

'No. I don't really have many friends at all. I've spent the last eight years travelling the world with Noah. Beyond him and my sisters, I don't have anyone.'

She chewed on her nacho thoughtfully. 'So you've never had a long-term relationship?'

'No.'

She stared at him as he scooped some guacamole onto his nacho. She understood that having a relationship would be tricky if Angel was moving around so much, but this felt like a choice more than anything else.

'Why is that?' Clover asked.

Angel frowned but just then the steaks arrived.

She shouldn't have asked that. It was none of her business. They were friends and she had no interest in making it something more than that and clearly neither did he. They were having some fun and he was helping her out. But there was something a little sad about going through life alone and as his friend she wondered if she could help him out too.

Angel took a bite of his steak and moaned with appreciation. 'God, I can see why you wanted to come here so much, this is amazing. I definitely have stiff competition tonight.'

Clover tucked into her steak and decided to let him change the subject. At least for now.

They were silent for a while as they ate and then Angel spoke.

'My mum died several years ago but she'd had Alzheimer's and dementia for a few years before that. She was so young and her memory deteriorated so quickly. She forgot most of what she'd done with her life, which just broke my heart because she'd had a full life and she simply had no recollection of it. She did remember her early life though, her late teens, she remembered that as vividly as if it had happened the day before. She was a ballet dancer, something I never knew until the very end of her life. She'd been in shows in the West End and Broadway before she hit her twenties. She'd been set for a glittering career and then she fell pregnant with me. My mum told me how gutted she was when she found out she was pregnant. She had no idea she was talking to me at this point, who I was, I think she just thought I was a nice man who would visit her. She told me it had been hard to find any love for me when I was born because I had ruined her life.'

'Shit, Angel, that must have been so hard to hear.'

Angel shook his head. 'Not really. My mum was not the mum I knew and loved towards the end, she was a very different person; snappy, angry at everything. It wasn't her fault. I couldn't really be hurt by the things she was saying or by the feelings she'd had when she was in her late teens, early twenties. I mean, yes of course it hurt a little to hear that, but my memories of growing up with my mum are all happy ones. She might not have loved me when I was born but that soon changed. There was not a day that went by when she didn't cuddle me and tell me she loved me. It was just me and her for the longest time. My dad was never in my life and I never missed him because Mum was everything I needed. She'd play football with me, make cakes, we'd go on holiday together; she was brilliant. Later, she met my stepdad and got married, had four beautiful daughters. We were all very happy together.'

Angel took another bite of his steak as he thought.

'One thing struck me about our conversations though. She regretted the life she had. I mean, I know she was very happy with my stepdad and our huge family and the grandkids, I don't think she regretted that at all. But when she was at the end of her life, she looked back on it with regret and I hated the thought of that. I hate the thought of getting to the end of my life and looking back and thinking I wished I'd done that. I don't have serious relationships because I worry I could be missing out on something amazing. I want to see the world, taste all the food, experience the cultures, meet people, and if I was to settle down now I wonder if I would look back on my life with regret for all the things I didn't do.'

Clover thought about that for a minute as she ate.

'Don't you think that although your life might be filled with wonderful sights and sounds, you might have other regrets; not falling in love, not spending the rest of your life with your soul mate, not being a father? I think you could miss out on a lot by denying yourself that.'

'Oh, I'm sure I'll settle down eventually, get married, have a couple of kids, but right now I want to explore every single pocket of the world so I can look back and say I did it all. No regrets.'

'What if you look back on your life and regret that you let one of these women go, that you missed out on being with the love of your life?'

He stared at her. 'I've never really thought about that before.'

'There's been no one that you thought about exploring more with?'

He didn't say anything and Clover felt her eyes widen in embarrassment. 'Oh god, I didn't mean me. I know what this is, I know you don't want that with me and I don't want that either. This is just two friends having fun. I just meant I'm sure there's been someone that you thought you'd like to get to know better.'

He focussed his attention on his steak for a moment. 'There was a time when I thought I'd never settle down, but lately I have thought about it. Occasionally.'

'There was someone?'

He paused. 'I meant that seeing Noah and Aria together, part of me wants what they have.'

Clover smiled. 'They are a walking advert for the happy ever after, aren't they?'

'Is that what you want?' Angel asked.

'Yes,' Clover said, without any hesitation. 'Eventually.'

Angel grinned. 'So you're not ready to settle down either?'

'You're forgetting that my last relationship was a shitty one and while we're now dating and will hopefully get to the sex part soon, I'm not sure if I want to commit to a proper relationship just yet. I think it will take me significantly longer to be ready for that.'

'I get that.'

'And I get where you're coming from too. I'm sorry if it sounded like I was judging you.'

'I didn't feel like you were judging me at all. I've never told anyone about my mum or my reasons for wanting to travel, so it feels good to discuss it with you. You have a way of making me see things in a different light. Another of the things I worry about is me getting dementia or Alzheimer's too. Doing all this and not being able to remember any of it. So I take pictures and videos of the important stuff, the memories I want to hold onto forever, so I can look back at my life and see it all again.'

'I like that idea.'

Clover suddenly remembered the photo he'd insisted on taking on their walk down to the village.

'You took a photo of me tonight, of us.'

His eyes widened a little, almost as if he regretted saying what he'd just said. 'That was just... I was just being silly.'

'Oh, right. Not one for the photo album then?'

'You giving me porno tongue? I might have to keep it for comedy value.'

Her heart dropped into her stomach, her defences suddenly raised as she had a sudden flashback to the night Marcus had betrayed her.

'I don't want you sharing those photos of me.'

His face fell. 'Clover, I would never do that—'

'Do you take photos of all the women you've slept with, so you can look back on all your conquests?'

He frowned. 'No, that would be a pretty seedy thing to do. I've never taken photos of any of the women I've been with. I don't mean this to sound disrespectful to any of those women, because they were all lovely women I had a good time with, but the things I take photos of are the kind of things that change your life, the wow moments, the breathtakingly amazing moments of wonder that you never ever want to forget.'

'So why did you take a photo of me?'

'Because you looked absolutely magnificent tonight, you took my breath away and I felt like the luckiest man alive to be with you. Because you make me happy in ways I've never felt before and I wanted to capture it.'

She stared at him in shock.

'Look at the photos,' Angel said, swiping the screen of his phone a few times. 'If you hate them, I'll delete them straightaway.'

She took the phone and looked at them. The camera had captured the two of them perfectly and even she had to admit she looked quite pretty. And Angel looked so utterly happy, in fact they both did.

'I'm being ridiculous, aren't I?' Clover said.

'No, not at all. After what Marcus did to you, I think it's

perfectly reasonable that you're a bit sensitive about having your photo taken.'

'Sorry. It was just when you said you were going to keep the photo for comedy value, I remembered what Marcus said when he threatened to share the video. He said everyone would laugh at me. What you said hit a raw nerve.'

'I'm sorry, I just didn't want to admit the truth about why I'd really taken that photo, it seemed a bit much for a second date. So I laughed it off instead and now I feel like an ass.'

'Well, if you're trying to score brownie points, telling me I look magnificent and that I took your breath away is a great place to start. I think you might get triple points for that.'

He grinned. 'I am sorry. Do you want me to delete them?'

'No, they're nice and I like that you might keep them and look back on them when you're old and grey.'

Angel took the phone back and they lapsed into silence for a while as they finished their steaks.

Clover thought about what he'd said about his love of travel and his current situation.

'So if you started working for Noah because it meant you could fulfil your dreams of travelling the world, what does that mean for you now he's retired?'

Angel lifted his empty plate to the edge of the table and picked up his glass of beer, taking a long drink. Eventually he spoke.

'I honestly don't know. I love working with Noah and I love it here on Jewel Island but... I didn't see myself settling down just yet. Buying myself a cottage overlooking the beach, being part of a population of around eight hundred people, that feels a bit small for my liking.'

'Will you leave?'

Clover didn't like the idea of that. She didn't want to lose Angel even if they were never going to be more than friends.

If he got a job somewhere else then it was quite likely she'd never see him again. She felt the ache in her chest at that thought.

'Maybe, I don't know,' he said. 'I'm quite happy where I am for the next few weeks or months, I've only just got back. But I don't know if this life will suit me in the long run. I guess we'll see. Do you ever think about travelling?'

'Of course, I'd love to see the world too. But on holiday for a few weeks here and there, not as part of a never-ending world tour. My life is here, my sisters, my animals, my hotel, the beautiful Jewel Island. I have my dream job teaching dance, my little cottage by Ruby Falls. I couldn't be happier.'

He nodded. 'I can appreciate that. You've found your place in life. I've never really had that. That pull to somewhere specific. But if you ever change your mind, you could come with me. I'm sure we'd have fun together.'

'That sounds great,' Clover said, knowing that would probably never happen. They wanted very different things.

'Where would you go, where would be first on your list?' he asked.

'Australia and New Zealand,' Clover said, without hesitation.

'Oh, you've thought about this?'

'Many times. I've been to Canada quite a bit with Skye and seen quite a few parts of America. I've visited some of the main parts of Europe but there's something about Australia and New Zealand that feel completely different. Like another world.'

'It is, especially New Zealand. We should definitely go sometime.'

She smiled. She wondered what it would be like to go on holiday with Angel, two friends who were pushing the boundaries of friendship. Going on holiday together didn't exactly sound casual, which was what they both wanted. She decided to change the subject slightly.

'Where's left for you? You must have done most of the world already.'

'There are a lot of places that haven't been on Noah's radar for buying and selling hotels. I've been to most of the world's major cities because that's where Noah normally does most of his business. A lot of the quieter places have eluded me. The Galapagos, for example. I'd love to go there.'

'Well if you ever go, you'll have to come back and tell me all about it.'

He stared at her as if he was coming to the same conclusion that she had. If he left, she didn't know if their short-lived friendship was strong enough to withstand not seeing each other again. She'd lived in London before moving back to Jewel Island to help her sisters run the hotel and she'd stayed in touch with her friends at first but after a while she had drifted apart from them. She was too far away from London for people to want to pop by for the weekend and she was always too busy with the hotel to make the trip up there. Besides, London had been tainted for her after what Marcus had done, she was quite happy to leave that part of her life behind. But she wasn't ready to let Angel go. They would just have to try extra hard to stay in touch.

Angel reached across the table to take her hand. 'You're not going to get rid of me that easily. I'll come back and visit.'

'And maybe I could fly out and spend a few days with you, wherever you end up in the world.'

'I'd like that.'

She smiled at him across the table. Making friends with Angel was one of the best things to ever happen to her. He was patient, kind, understanding. He was pretty bloody magnificent himself.

CHAPTER FOURTEEN

Angel held Clover's hand as they walked through the village, which had taken on a much more sinister appearance than the sweet Halloween fair he'd seen before. The costumes had been amped up so they looked hideous and terrifying rather than cute. All the horror film characters were prowling the streets, from Freddy Krueger, Pennywise, Michael Myers, Chucky and several hooded *Scream* characters. There was someone juggling axes, a magician throwing knives at her assistant and a man chasing people with a chainsaw, which for health and safety reasons Angel hoped wasn't a real one. Instead of innocent childish laughter, the air was filled with screams of terror as the hotel guests and the villagers subjected themselves to be petrified to death.

This was certainly not the ideal end to a romantic date, but then again he'd never done any kind of dating before so he wasn't really sure what the perfect end to a perfect date would be. He'd pictured it being a lot quieter and more tranquil than this and with probably a lot more kissing. Although maybe this was a better option. He was quite happy to date Clover, have some fun with her, but he didn't need to make it super romantic and make it more than it was between them.

Although he'd already done that with the comments he'd made earlier about her taking his breath away.

She looked up at him, her face filled with laughter and happiness, and he felt an ache in his chest.

Except he wanted to give her that romance. She wanted the happy ever after and, although he couldn't give her that, he wanted her to have everything but: romantic gestures, candles, flowers. She'd said she just wanted a normal relationship and if this was anyone else but him they'd be pulling out all the stops to impress her right now.

He stroked a finger down her cheek. 'Shall we go for a walk on the beach?'

'Oh, that would be lovely.'

They walked across the green, avoiding most of the mayhem, but they were stopped by Sylvia O'Hare before they could get to the steps that led down to the beach.

'This is all a bit exciting, isn't it,' Sylvia said, gesturing to the carnage going on around them.

'Is this more up your street than the daytime activities?' Clover asked.

'I was just chased by a big muscly man brandishing a sword and wearing nothing but a kilt. I was very tempted to let him catch me.'

Angel laughed.

Sylvia's eyes cast down to where they were holding hands and then looked over her shoulder in the direction they were heading. 'Going to the beach?'

'We thought we'd take a short walk,' Clover said.

'How romantic,' Sylvia waggled her eyebrows mischievously. 'You know, I lost my virginity on a beach. Great big Viking of a man called Erik. He had a bushy beard which made things very interesting, let me tell you. I ended up writing *The Pirate's Passion* based on that night, one of my bestsellers. My friends all had crappy losing-their-virginity stories, but mine was tremendous. Actually, my fourth husband made love to me for the first time on a beach too. Ah Jimmy, he was a complete sod, slept with loads of women while we were married, but my god he was good in the bedroom. Or out of it, if you know what I mean. He loved outdoor sex. There's something wildly romantic about having sex on the beach. You two should give it a go.'

'We'll bear that in mind,' Clover said.

Sylvia patted her shoulder and gave Angel a wink. 'Well, have a good night.'

She moved off but, as Angel and Clover walked away, Sylvia called out again.

'Angel, could I just have a quick word?' Sylvia said.

Angel looked at Clover in confusion but she gestured for him to go ahead.

He jogged over to where Sylvia was waiting for him.

'Here,' Sylvia said, pressing something into his hand and closing his fingers over the top of it before he could see what it was. She gave him another wink and then hurried off.

He opened his hand and burst out laughing. He moved back over to Clover and showed her the bright pink condom.

Clover laughed and her laughter got louder as she looked more closely at it. 'And it's bubble-gum flavoured too.'

Angel shook his head with a smirk and shoved it into his jeans pocket.

'Wait, why are you keeping it?' Clover laughed in shock. 'If you think I'm going to be sleeping with you for the first time on the beach where anyone can see us, with a pink flavoured condom, you've got another think coming.'

'Well I didn't think that, it's only our second date after all. Maybe we'll save that for our third date.'

Clover laughed and playfully swatted him.

'It's also a bit cold for outdoor sex tonight, I'd be fearful some important bits might snap off.'

'That's true.'

'I'm putting it in my pocket because there are no bins here and I don't fancy going back to the fair over there in case Sylvia collars me again and gives me a vibrator next time. And I'm not a litterbug, so I'm not throwing it away.'

Clover smiled, taking his hand again, as they went down the steps onto Diamond Sands. 'Fair point. You're a lot more wholesome than I imagined.'

'I'll take that as a compliment.'

They stepped into the darkness, away from the noise and the lights of the fair, the cool sand beneath their feet. It was much quieter here, the gentle lap of the waves on the shore now the most prominent sound, the moon casting silvery ribbons across the water.

She pulled him to a stop and stroked his face. 'You should. You're making this whole thing very easy for me.'

'Oh well, that's not exactly a hardship for me. I love spending time with you and making you smile.'

She smiled and then leaned up and kissed him. He cupped her face and kissed her back. If there was a perfect end to a date, it would be this. And surprisingly the warmth that filled his chest as he held her didn't bother him at all.

Clover smiled as she looked down at her hand entwined with Angel's as they walked through the lit-up gardens back to her cottage. There was something so wonderful and delicious about holding hands with Angel Mazzeo. They fitted together perfectly. She'd started off just wanting some fun with him, to date and kiss and make love just like a normal person would with no expectations of it ever being more than that. But now she was starting to think she might want more, which was ridiculous. Angel didn't do settling down and she really wasn't sure if she was ready for a proper serious relationship just yet. But she didn't want this to end anytime soon either. Though what happened if it went on for months and she found herself falling in love with him? What would happen when he left to continue his travels around the world? Would she go with him, would he even want her to?

She sighed. Why was she jumping so far ahead? She should just enjoy what they had now. Angel could end the whole thing in a few days or weeks. He wasn't known for his longevity.

'What are you thinking about?' Angel asked, interrupting her thoughts.

'You, us,' Clover said, honestly, as they approached her cottage.

'All good, I hope?'

She leaned up and kissed him briefly on the lips. 'All good right now.'

He frowned slightly but she kissed him again before letting them into the house.

Orion immediately came to greet them, wrapping himself around both their legs before stalking off to his favourite place on the sofa.

She hung her coat up as Angel was taking off his own.

'Thank you for tonight, I had so much fun,' Clover said, heading for the kitchen.

'It was my pleasure.'

'Would you like a hot chocolate?' she said.

'Oh yes, that sounds nice. I'll get the fire started.'

Clover giggled. 'For someone who likes life fast-paced, you're a bit of a grandad sometimes, drinking a hot chocolate, sitting by the fire.'

'Wow, that makes me feel old. I'll just go and get my pipe and slippers.'

Clover laughed and walked into the kitchen. She came back a few minutes later to find a fire roaring away and Angel studying the photos on the mantelpiece. She moved over to him, handing him his mug and running a hand down his back. She realised he was looking at a photo of her dad who had died the year before. Her dad was holding up a fishing rod and the tiniest fish in the world. He had the biggest smile on his face.

'I'm sorry I never got to meet your dad, by all accounts he was a wonderful man. Noah speaks very highly of him,' Angel said.

'He was amazing. My mum died when me and Skye were only ten and he raised us all by himself. He was a brilliant man who had the biggest heart.'

'Runs in the family.'

She smiled.

His attention moved to a small wire statue of a horse that looked like it was running flat out, its mane and tail flying in the wind.

'This is incredible,' Angel said, carefully picking it up.

'It's from New York. My mum fell in love with it when she and my dad were on holiday there. They'd only been dating a few months at that point. They didn't buy it, but she was a wonderful artist and she kept drawing it over the next few weeks after they'd come home. Neither of them could remember the name of the shop but somehow Dad managed to track it down and get it shipped over because she loved it so much. Mum said she knew then that he loved her. He'd gone to so much trouble just to make her happy. It was a symbol of his love for her. They got married a few months later.'

'I like that,' Angel said.

'I suppose ultimately, eventually, I want what they had. The forever kind of love.'

Angel put the statue down. 'I guess I want that too… eventually.'

That surprised her. 'Really?' Clover took a sip from her hot chocolate.

'Yes of course. If I was to give up the life I lead, it'd have to be for someone incredible, someone I don't actually want to leave, someone who spending time with would be more important than going anywhere or doing anything else. Someone I love with every fibre of my body. I'm not going to settle for anything less.'

She smiled. 'It sounds like you have your priorities right after all.'

'Just because I'm not looking for that right now, doesn't mean I don't want that, when the time is right.'

'Sadly I don't think there is a timetable for love. It comes along at the most inconvenient of times.'

'Maybe. But I think if that all-consuming love came along, I probably wouldn't think it inconvenient at all.'

She smiled; she liked that.

Maybe Angel wasn't destined to spend the rest of his life alone after all. Maybe one day he would find that special someone he wanted forever with.

She ignored the kick of jealousy that came with that thought.

～

Angel lay in his bed, wide awake with the moonlight streaming through the windows. He picked up his phone and started scanning through his photos, which was something he normally did if he was having trouble sleeping. He'd look through his favourite places and sights, trying to imprint them all on his brain. If he was feeling particularly awake, he'd edit the latest ones into a short video and upload them onto YouTube for posterity.

He didn't normally have a lot of trouble sleeping, unless he had jet lag or something was bothering him. But the reason he was wide awake now at three in the morning was curled up against his chest, her blonde hair splayed out behind her on the bed, her breathing heavy as she slept.

One of the greatest sights he had ever seen was Niagara Falls. On a boat trip to the bottom of the falls, he'd looked up and seen the sheer volume of water thundering down to the river below and just felt nothing but wonder at the tremendous power of nature. And in many ways, what he was feeling now was the same feeling. A sense of excitement for what was happening between them. It was something wonderful and he had the same buzz in his veins that he had when he was going to see some amazing place that he'd wanted to see for a long time. He had no idea what was going to happen between him and Clover, whether they had any kind of future together and whether he even wanted that, but he was glad he was here now, being with her, being a part of whatever was happening between them. It made him happy.

As he scrolled through the photos, he came across the ones he'd taken that night of him and Clover together, kissing, and it made his heart leap. He stared at them together. This thing was not like anything he'd ever experienced before. He had a special folder in his phone for the photos that meant the most to him and, before he thought any more about it, he selected those photos of him and Clover and moved them to that folder. If something made him feel this good, then it definitely deserved a place in that folder.

He glanced down at her and smiled. Clover's hair was over her face, her breath a whisper across his skin, her hand resting over his heart.

He held up the camera and took a photo of himself, being careful not to get her in the shot. He would never take a photo of her without her consent, especially not after her reaction to those other photos tonight, but he was quite happy to take a photo of himself. He looked at the screen and saw the huge grin on his face. He had filled his life with moments that took his breath away and this was definitely one of them. He pointed off camera towards Clover as he took the photo and he hoped with everything he had, if the time came in his life where he had trouble remembering his past, he would look at this photo and still remember what it was that made him so damned, ridiculously happy

CHAPTER FIFTEEN

Clover was on her way back from her Wednesday morning tap dancing class when Aria caught up with her.

'Hey, how was your date last night?'

Clover smiled. 'Wonderful. We had amazing steak, we talked, we laughed, we kissed, we went for a walk on the beach, we slept in the same bed together. As dates go, it was pretty bloody spectacular. I really like him.'

'Is it more than that?' Aria asked.

Clover took a long drink from her water bottle and then shook her head. 'No, this is all lovely and I feel like I'm finally ready for this again – dating, making love with someone kind and patient – but I'm not ready for something more. There's a big difference between what me and Angel are doing and settling down, getting married and having babies. It's going to take a lot more time for me to be ready to trust someone enough for a long-term relationship. And someone really special too.'

'You don't think Angel is special enough?' Aria said, as they walked towards Clover's office.

'Oh god he is, definitely, but he's also—'

'Sitting at your desk,' Tilly quickly interrupted as she could see into Clover's office from where she was standing at reception.

Clover mouthed a thank you to Tilly and peered round her office door. Angel turned round and grinned at her, before returning his attention to his laptop.

'We're sharing an office now?' Clover said.

'Well, we're already sharing a bed,' Angel said.

Clover glanced at Aria, who couldn't disguise the smile on her face.

'I'll leave you to it,' Aria said and walked off.

Clover moved into the office and she couldn't help smiling at Angel too. He was wearing a t-shirt with a mummified Mickey Mouse today.

'I quite like it in here, it's quiet, it has nice views and the company is second to none,' he said.

Clover moved round to sit in her own chair and switched on her computer.

'You never finished what you were going to say,' Angel said, an easy smile on his face. 'You said I was special but also… also what?'

Clover had been going to say that Angel was seemingly a complete tart when it came to women and had worse commitment issues than she did. She might have to soften that a bit before saying it to him.

She cleared her throat. 'I was going to say that you're also not looking for a proper relationship either.'

He studied her for a moment and then nodded. 'That's true.'

She checked her emails. 'Oh, the photographer has sent through the photos from our wedding shoot.'

'Ooh, let me look,' Angel said, wheeling his chair round to

her side of the desk, sitting so close his glorious scent washed over her and she could feel the warmth from his body.

She clicked them open and Angel leaned closer to her to see them.

The first one was of them cutting the fake cake. Clover was impressed, it genuinely looked like a real wedding photo. Brian had captured it beautifully.

'Wow,' Angel laughed. 'That looks amazing. We look like a real couple.'

She clicked through them, seeing the ones of their first dance together, exchanging rings, sharing an ice cream in Cones at the Cove, walking through the gardens, overlooking the sea, standing on Sapphire Bay. Next to her Angel drew quiet, the smile fading from his face, and she thought she knew why. One thing that shone from every photo was the affection and adoration they felt for each other. It wasn't just the smiles that Brian had directed them to have, it was so much more than that. They'd both fancied each other ever since they'd met, but these photos showed it was more than that too. Well, certainly from her point of view, it looked like she was completely in love with him, which was just silly. She didn't like Angel in that way. Oh god, if he saw how she was looking at him, he might back-pedal away from their tentative relationship. He didn't want serious, but these photos looked pretty bloody serious to her.

'Christ,' Angel muttered. 'I feel like we're staring at our future.'

She looked at him. 'A future neither of us want.'

He stared at her for the longest time. 'Of course, yes. I mean, this is all for show.'

He was still quiet as she clicked through more of the photos. There were some gorgeous ones of them standing by the waterfalls, the beautiful scarlet and gold maple trees as a stunning backdrop. But Clover could barely concentrate on them as she knew what was coming next.

Sure enough, as she clicked through to the next photos, there she was kissing Angel. Some of them were sweet, some were passionate but she couldn't take her eyes off the images.

'Best first kiss ever,' Angel said, softly.

She swallowed a lump of emotion that clogged in her throat.

She stopped on one photo where they were kissing but smiling against each other's lips. Angel was cupping her face and looking at her with such affection.

She stared at it, her heart thundering in her chest, unable to look away. Because despite what she had told Aria and Angel, despite what she had told herself, she suddenly wanted that more than anything.

Angel was busy preparing some Facebook ads for the hotel, pushing it for the lead-up to Christmas. As soon as the Halloween festival was finished, they would be all systems go for Christmas: parties, festive meals, even lunch with Santa. They needed to get the adverts ready now to try to get the bookings in for late November.

He glanced over at Clover who was busy working at her own computer. Somehow, they had managed to be professional and choose which of the wedding photos worked best for the brochure and website without any emotional attachment to any of the photos.

And if he kept telling himself that he might actually believe it.

They hadn't said much since then and he felt like he needed to clear the air between them.

'Are you OK?' Angel asked.

Clover looked up at him and nodded, before returning her attention to her computer.

So, probably not OK.

She let out a big sigh and turned back to him. 'I feel like I'm going to lose you over this.'

He felt his eyebrows shoot up. 'That is never going to happen.'

'I feel like we're just playing at being in a relationship, and what happens when it all comes to an end? Do you honestly think we'll still be friends?'

'Yes I do,' Angel said, without hesitation.

'So we'll just carry on as we are for the next few weeks, we'll have sex, and then in a few weeks' or months' time one of us will end it because we've had enough and we'll just go back to being friends again? You don't think that one or both of us could get hurt from this?'

If anyone was going to get hurt by this it would be him, but he could handle that. He couldn't handle hurting her.

'I hope to god I never do anything to hurt you, but I thought we were both coming at this from the same page, that we both wanted something casual, fun, no strings.'

'What if one of us has turned the page?'

She'd obviously seen how he'd looked at her in those photos. For a man who'd spent a lot of time playing cards over the years, it seemed he had no poker face when it came to her.

'You don't need to worry about that,' Angel said.

'I don't?'

'It's not going to get weird between us.'

'I think we're already there,' Clover said.

'You want to stop this before we go any further?'

'No. God, no I definitely don't want that… Do you?'

'Absolutely not.'

They stared at each other.

'I'm enjoying myself way too much to want to stop this,' Angel said.

'Me too.'

'And if it gets weird we'll deal with it then. I'm sure we can be mature about it and I'm pretty bloody confident that we can still be friends when it's all over because there's no way I'm losing you.'

A slow, cautious smile spread across her face. 'OK.'

'OK?'

She nodded.

'We're still on for our date tonight?' he asked.

'Yes, definitely, I want to see what you have planned.'

'Ah, I think you'll love it.'

There was a knock on the office door and Angel turned round to see Noah there.

'Can I borrow you for a second?' Noah asked Angel.

'Sure.'

He stood up, flashing Clover a wink as he walked out and she smiled at him, which filled him with some relief.

Angel followed Noah into his office and Noah closed the door, before moving round to the other side of his desk.

'So I've been thinking about the future and you and...' his boss started.

'Wait, are you proposing to me? Because I'm not sure what Aria would say about that.'

Noah grinned. 'I don't think I'll be lowering my standards that much. But this is something serious so I'd appreciate if you can shut your face for a moment.'

Angel smirked and then zipped his lips closed as he took a seat.

'It goes without saying, you will always have a job here, god knows we need you for all the marketing, website, general dogsbody stuff. The last eight years my company has gone from strength to strength but I couldn't have done any of it without you.'

'Christ, another compliment. Are you dying?' Angel said.

'I thought you were going to shut up.'

'Sorry.'

'Look, my life is here now and I have no intention of ever leaving. That part of my life, travelling around the world, buying and selling hotels, is over, and I'm very happy to spend my days walking on the beach with Aria, adopt a few kids, pop out a few more, get a dog but... I know that's not what you want.'

'Oh, you don't need to worry about me, I'll be fine,' Angel said. He had no idea what he was going to do, but he had no intention of making up his mind or leaving just yet, he was having far too much fun with Clover.

'Well, I had a thought. What if you were to carry on the company in my place? I'd provide the funds, but it would be you that handles everything, you'd be the man on the ground, arranging all the renovations to your specifications, organising the staff, pushing the hotel to be better, negotiating the sale. I'd be on the other end of the phone or email if you wanted advice but generally it would be your baby. I'd obviously pay you more or we could come up with an arrangement for a large percentage of the sale.'

Angel stared at him. 'Are you serious?'

'You've done most of this stuff for me over the years in one way or another, admittedly not all at the same time, but you have experience in all of it. I know you'll do a great job.'

This was an amazing opportunity, but it was one thing being told what to do and then making it happen, it was another thing altogether making the decisions himself.

But this was the answer to all his problems. He didn't have

to give up working with Noah, and he still got to travel the world. He could also come back to Jewel Island on a regular basis and see Clover too.

It was a lot of pressure to take Noah's money and make a success of it though. 'I don't know the first thing about renovating a hotel, about what looks good and what doesn't.'

'I think you know a lot more than you think you do. Listen, you don't have to decide now. I'd totally understand if you're happy to stay here, but there's a hotel in Rome I've had my eye on for a while. I know the owner quite well and he's told me that he plans to sell it. He's giving me first dibs on it before it goes on the market in a few weeks. You could fly out, spend a week or two there, have a look at it, decide if it's something you want to get your teeth into. If not then he'll put it up for sale, no big deal. But we need to move relatively quickly on this. I think once it goes up for sale it will get snapped up straightaway so we need to make a decision before that happens.'

Angel nodded. 'OK, I'm happy to have a look at least. When would you need me to go?'

'Ideally, I'd want you to go Saturday. There's a big wedding there on Sunday, there'll be lots of guests and I think it would be good for you to see the hotel at its busiest. Also, if you're keen, we could arrange for you to view some other hotels in other places too, that way you can choose the best one for you.'

Angel thought about it for a moment. Leaving on Saturday didn't give him much time with Clover. He'd been having fun with her but it felt like they were just at the beginning of something wonderful. He'd made a commitment to be there for her as long as she needed him but if they really were just having fun then this felt like too good an opportunity to pass up. He kind of wanted to talk to her about it first.

'Can I tell you tomorrow?'

Noah shrugged. 'Of course.'

Angel sighed. His nice romantic date that night was now looking less and less romantic.

Clover pushed the door open on Cones at the Cove and rushed over to Skye and Jesse who were waiting in one of the booths. The place was closed for a few hours before it would reopen in the evening but Noah had just sent her and Skye a text asking to meet with them. He wouldn't say what it was about but they were under strict instructions not to tell Aria.

'What's going on?' Clover said, pulling off her scarf and sitting down.

'I have no idea,' Skye said, passing Clover a mug of hot chocolate with whipped cream and marshmallows on the top. 'But I thought we might need fortification.'

Clover took a sip of the sweet velvety chocolatiness and noticed it was banoffee flavoured, one of her favourites.

'What if he wants to buy back our share of the hotel?' Skye said.

'He can't do that,' Jesse said. 'You all legally own twenty-five percent of the hotel; he has no greater say in what happens to the hotel than either of you. He can offer to buy you out, of course, but you don't have to accept.'

'I just don't like this sneaking around behind Aria's back, why can't he tell her too, whatever it is,' Skye said.

'I know,' Clover said. 'They are supposed to be partners, in every sense of the word, he shouldn't have secrets from her.'

'I think we just need to stay calm and hear him out,' Jesse said. 'Noah seems like a great bloke and I'm sure he has his reasons not to involve Aria in this chat. Let's just give him a chance to explain.'

Clover nodded, thoughtfully, and then a thought struck her.

'What if it's something to do with the adoption?' she said. 'What if something has gone wrong? Aria will be gutted if she can't adopt, she's always wanted to do that.'

'But there are several adoption agencies in this country, aren't there?' Skye said. 'If there is a problem with this one then Aria can go to a different agency. I know she'll have to start the process all over again but she doesn't have to give up.'

'True, but it would still be a huge blow.'

'Let's not jump to conclusions,' Jesse said. 'It might not be something bad.'

'Well, we're about to find out,' Clover muttered, gesturing to the door as Noah had just walked in. He looked nervous.

He came over and smiled at them, but it was a forced smile. He sat down next to Clover and pulled his gloves off.

'Um, thank you for coming at such short notice,' Noah said, his fingers restlessly playing with one of his gloves. 'Um... Jesse, would you mind giving us a minute, this is kind of a private matter.'

Jesse made a move to leave but Skye held him back. 'Whatever you want to say to us, you can say in front of Jesse, I have no secrets from him.'

Noah frowned. 'It doesn't really concern Jesse...'

Skye folded her arms defiantly and Noah nodded in defeat.

'And we have to say, we don't like this secret meeting malarkey. Aria should be here too,' Skye said.

Clover nodded. 'She loves you, I think she'd be upset if she felt you had secrets from her, things you couldn't discuss with her.'

Noah cleared his throat. 'It wouldn't be appropriate to have her here.'

'Why not?' Skye said, in exasperation.

'I'd rather she didn't know.'

'But—' Clover started but Noah held his hand up.

'Please, I think there might have been some misunderstanding. I'm sorry for the secrecy but... I intend to ask Aria to marry me and I'd like to do the traditional thing of asking her family for their blessing. With your parents not being around anymore, I'd like to ask you two.'

Skye and Clover stared at him in shock. Jesse let out a bark of a laugh and then kissed Skye on the cheek. 'I don't think you need me here to help you handle this one. Noah, congratulations, I hope you'll be very happy together.'

With that, Jesse unfolded his giant frame from the booth and sauntered off into the kitchen.

'You're going to propose?' Clover said, finding her voice at last.

'Yes. I love your sister, she is my entire world. And I know we had a bit of a shaky start to our relationship but I hope I've made up for that in the last six months. She makes me so happy and I want to spend the rest of my life making her happy too.'

Skye let out a laugh of relief. 'Oh my god, I wasn't expecting that.'

'Well, I have to say, I'm going to propose anyway, but it would be nice to know I have your support.'

'Of course you have our support,' Clover laughed. 'I have never seen her so happy as she is when she's with you. I can't believe you're going to get married, this is wonderful news.'

'Thank you,' Noah said and then turned his attention to Skye.

Skye got up from the table and walked round and gave

Noah a big hug. 'I'm delighted for you both and more than a little relieved. Welcome to the family.'

Noah laughed in relief. 'Thank you. She has to say yes first.'

'She will,' Skye said, sitting back down.

'When do you plan on doing it?' Clover said, needing the details.

'Friday, at the lantern walk through the gardens.'

'Oh my god that's two days away,' Clover squealed. 'Do you need our help, can we do anything?'

Noah laughed. 'No, I have it all covered, I have a big speech and the ring, so...'

'Well, if you want to run the speech by us, we can tell you if it works,' Clover said, hopefully.

'I might keep that one a surprise for Aria,' Noah said. 'Can I rely on you two to keep this between us until then?'

Skye zipped her lips closed and Clover crossed her heart. 'Our lips are sealed.'

CHAPTER SIXTEEN

Clover had been told to wait in her bedroom while Angel prepared for their date. She had no idea what he was going to do but she couldn't smell any cooking going on and she was starving.

She felt better about what was happening between them after their conversation earlier. She was just going to enjoy it for what it was and not worry about the future. Those wedding photos didn't mean anything, not really, they were just two people who liked each other a lot playing a part.

She was having fun with Angel; she didn't need to over-complicate things with feelings and what ifs.

There was a knock on her bedroom door.

She opened it and Angel was waiting for her, holding out his arm. She grinned and took it, following him down the stairs.

'I'm excited to see what you have planned, hope it involves food,' Clover said, her stomach rumbling.

'I've got you covered there, you don't need to worry,' Angel said and then, to her surprise, he offered out her coat.

'We're going out?'

Angel had been a while preparing for the date, so she'd assumed that they would be staying in. She'd kind of hoped for an evening in with just the two of them, no interruptions.

'Not far, I promise,' Angel said and then escorted her outside.

At the bottom of the garden, near to the falls, a fire was burning merrily away. There were blankets and cushions around the fire and there were little jam jars filled with candles dotted around the lawn. It looked magical.

Clover moved closer and could see there was plenty of food on the blankets, they were clearly having a picnic. There was even a bottle of sparkling wine chilling in a bucket of ice.

'This is lovely, thank you.'

She sat down next to the fire, feeling the warmth of the golden flames. Angel sat down next to her as he poured out two glasses of wine that fizzed and frothed in the champagne flutes.

'Here's to... having fun,' he said, passing her a glass. She chinked her glass against his and took a drink, the bubbles dancing across her tongue.

She watched the flames twist and turn as she popped a grape in her mouth.

He reached out a hand and stroked his fingers through her hair. She looked at him and then leaned forward and kissed him. This man definitely knew how to kiss, he was slow and confident and undeniably sexy. And as the kiss continued, she found herself lying down on the soft blankets with Angel half on top of her. God, she wanted this man so much, if he was to make love to her here, now, by the side of the fire, she wouldn't even try to stop him. Although that was seemingly not the problem. His hands caressed her face, shoulders, her arms, her waist but never strayed any lower than that.

It almost felt silly to not be taking that step with him. She'd known him for six months, by rights they should have started dating back then but she'd held back. She didn't want to hold back anymore. Most importantly, she trusted him. He had been nothing but patient, kind and understanding throughout all of this. She knew he would never hurt her, at least not in the way that Marcus had. There was no reason to let the past stand in her way any longer.

She was just about to say that when her stomach gurgled noisily. Angel laughed against her lips and then pulled back slightly.

'I should probably let you eat and I… I need to talk to you about something too.' Angel sat up.

'Oh, that sounds interesting,' Clover said, feeling slightly disappointed that the moment had passed.

'I'm not sure you'll find it interesting but let's eat first, we can chat later.'

Clover sat up, finding that even more intriguing. She helped herself to some of the food and for a while they ate and chatted about nothing much, but she realised that he was nervous and she guessed it was something to do with what he wanted to talk to her about.

'OK, come on, out with it, you're making me nervous now,' Clover said, after she had finished off a slice of chocolate cake.

Angel put his plate down. 'So… I've been offered a job. Noah's job actually. He wants me to carry on his business without him. He'll provide the funds and I'd take care of everything else. I'd oversee the renovations, the staff, the sale, it would all be down to me.'

'Wow, that's amazing,' Clover said. 'What a brilliant opportunity for you.'

He cocked his head as he looked at her. 'You think so?'

She frowned. 'Of course.'

'If I was to take it, I'd be travelling a lot.'

'Well that's what you want, isn't it...' she trailed off as the reality of that hit her. She'd been so happy for her friend that she hadn't realised what it would mean for her. If Angel was continuing Noah's business, he'd be gone for months at a time. The chances of them having any kind of proper relationship would be zero. The chances right now were pretty low, and she wasn't even sure if she wanted that, but if he was here all the time, it was possible that he might start having feelings for her too, feelings that went way beyond friends with benefits. It was possible that she might be brave enough to take that leap with him, if she had enough time to let her guard down. It didn't look like that was going to happen now. 'When would you leave?'

'Noah has his eye on a hotel in Rome. He'd like me to go and have a look at it before it goes on the market to see if I'm interested in taking it over. He'd ideally like me there on Saturday.'

Her heart crashed into her stomach. When Angel had mentioned the new job, she'd presumed it wouldn't start for a few months or more, once they'd found a hotel and the sale had all gone through. She'd had no idea that Angel would be leaving in three days. The possibility of seeing where their relationship was going to go was suddenly out of the window.

'Wow, that's... three days. And you'd miss the ball.'

'I know. I kind of thought I'd have a few months at home at least.'

That was the second time that Angel had called Jewel Island home, but how could it be when he had no intention of staying?

'How long will you be gone?'

'Two weeks to start with, but Noah has said he might find

some other hotels for me to have a look at too, so it could be a month or more.'

Christ, this was the end before they'd barely even started. Tears pricked Clover's eyes and she was grateful for the darkness that meant he couldn't see her that well.

He was looking at her as if he was seeking her permission, as if he wanted her to say it was OK.

She cleared her throat. 'Well, that sounds like a lot of fun, you can't pass that up.'

He watched her for a moment. 'You think I should go?'

'Yes, absolutely,' Clover said, absently rubbing the ache in her chest. 'I mean, there's nothing for you here.'

She thought she saw a flash of hurt cross his face when she said that but it was gone as soon as it appeared, leaving her wondering if she had imagined it.

'No, of course not,' Angel said and she was surprised how much *that* hurt.

They sat in silence for a while and suddenly it felt awkward.

She glanced across at him and saw his jaw was tense. She reached out and stroked the back of his hand. 'I'm going to miss having fun with you though.'

He turned to her, his face softening. 'I'm going to miss that too.'

She leaned over and kissed him, stroking his face.

He pulled back slightly. 'I don't have to go.'

'Oh no, you have to, you can't miss out on that opportunity for me.'

He kissed her softly on the cheek, and then on her neck. 'Why not?'

His hot mouth on her skin made all coherent thoughts go out of her head. God, she wanted him to kiss her like that all over.

'Because...' she closed her eyes as he moved his mouth down towards her shoulder. 'Because you don't change the course of your life for someone you're just having fun with.'

'No, I don't suppose you do,' Angel said, still layering kisses across her neck.

Suddenly she made a snap decision.

'Well, I think we should make the most of the time we have left,' Clover said. She stood up and held out a hand for him.

He looked at her in confusion. 'What did you have in mind?'

She smiled. 'I think you know exactly what I have in mind.'

He stared at her with wide eyes for a moment and then scrabbled to his feet.

'Clover, I want that, of course I do. I've been thinking about what it would be like to make love to you for the last few months, but I don't think this is the right time. We don't need to step on the accelerator here, just because I'm leaving, we need to do this when you're ready. You don't really want to do this.'

'I do. And not just because you're leaving. When we were kissing, before we ate, I wanted it then. But more importantly, I need to do this. I've made it into this really big deal and I think I just need to get it over and done with.'

'Wow, that's the most romantic thing anyone has ever said to me,' Angel said dryly and she laughed.

'You know what I mean. I just want to be normal again, I just want to make love to you and to look forward to that like we're in a regular healthy relationship, not one where you're holding back.'

'I'm quite happy to hold back until you're ready,' Angel said.

'Well I'm not, we're doing it.'

Angel stared at her for a moment. 'OK, what can I do to make this easier for you?'

'Fully clothed would help,' Clover teased.

'We can do that, to a certain extent.'

'Or in complete darkness.'

'We can do that too.'

She thought about it for a moment. 'OK, yes, lights off.'

Angel nodded and then took her by the hand and led her back in the house.

She quickly dumped her coat as soon as she got back inside and Angel slipped out of his, watching her the whole time. He came back to her and kissed her, stroking her face.

She wondered if he would make love to her here, against the wall, or on her sofa, or on the floor in front of the fire. Either option was tantalising and exciting.

But he did neither of those things. He took her hand and led her up the stairs into her bedroom, as if he knew she'd be more comfortable in her own room. He left her standing by the door, as he closed the blinds and the curtains. She normally only did that in the middle of winter to keep some of the warmth in.

He fished a condom out of his pocket and placed it on the bedside drawers, then he came over to her and closed the door softly behind her. He cupped her face in his hands, kissing her softly, and she felt herself melt in his arms.

'Are you sure you want this?' he whispered.

She nodded.

'Then let's get it over with,' Angel said, his mouth quirking up into a smirk.

He leaned over behind her and snapped off the light, plunging them into complete and utter darkness.

Her breath hitched with excitement and fear over what was going to happen next. But for once, excitement won out.

She wanted to enjoy this more than she wanted to run away from it.

Angel cupped her face and kissed her again, so tenderly that she couldn't help but smile. Not being able to see him made her other senses like smell and touch feel heightened.

She rested her hands on his chest for a moment, feeling the warmth of him on her fingers. She moved her hands to the buttons of his shirt and fumbled to undo them, but his hands stalled her work.

'I know you want to do this as quickly as possible but that doesn't mean we're not going to do this properly,' Angel said, his breath warm against her cheek. 'Let me take care of this.'

She frowned slightly, not sure if she wanted to give full control over to him, but as he placed a soft, reverential kiss on her neck, she knew she would let him do anything. She trusted this man completely.

His fingers caressed down her arms in no more than a whisper and then he linked hands with her as he continued to pepper kisses across her cheeks and neck. He was in no rush at all, whereas her body was thrumming with need and he'd barely touched her.

He moved one hand to her waist and a finger to her cheek, trailing it down, tracing it over her lips and down her neck, following the V of her dress down to just above her breast. She quivered under his touch.

'I'd really like to kiss you all over,' Angel said.

Christ, Clover swallowed a lump in her throat at that thought.

'I'd really like that too.'

He slid his hands round her back and slowly undid the zip of her dress. He moved his mouth to her neck as he slid the straps off her shoulders. She felt the dress slither to the floor. His hands touched across her skin, tentatively at first and then with more need. He gently removed her bra. Every touch, every movement was careful, considered, taking his time. He kissed her, softly taking her breasts in his hands, and she gasped against his lips. He paused and his hands dropped away but it wasn't fear or nerves that made her gasp, it was need. She took his hands and placed them firmly back over her breasts. He didn't need any more encouragement than that as he caressed them, sliding his thumb over her nipples as she arched into him.

He moved his hands down to her waist and then slowly slid her knickers down so she was completely naked. She waited for the awareness of her vulnerability, for all those fears to come thundering back, but as Angel wrapped his arms around her and held her close, kissing her sweetly, those fears never came.

Without taking his mouth from hers, he bent and lifted her into his arms and carried her to the bed, laying her down gently.

He stepped back and, as her eyes became more accustomed to the dark, she saw his shadow quickly undressing before he joined her on the bed, taking her back into his arms and kissing her again. He didn't take it any further than that for the longest time, kissing her, stroking her until she felt so relaxed she thought she could melt right into the bed.

His mouth started exploring her body, his hot lips adoring her, caressing across her skin, kissing everywhere until her body was crying out for more.

He slowly moved his hand between her legs, his touch gentle and teasing, almost a whisper against her most sensitive area and it immediately made her moan.

'Is this OK?' he asked.

'Yes, god, yes,' Clover said, moving closer to his fingers in desperate need.

She saw him grin in the darkness as he gave her exactly what she wanted. She didn't know whether it was because it had been so long since the last time she'd been touched like this or whether Angel had some magic touch but it felt like mere seconds before she was shouting out his name, trembling in his arms.

God, she wanted this man so much, her body craving his as he leaned over to grab the condom. She felt him fumble around and then heard him swear under his breath.

'Sorry, I've dropped the condom on the floor,' Angel said. 'And I can't find it.'

Clover burst out laughing.

'Not what I expected to hear from someone as smooth as you.'

She heard him chuckle. 'I've never done this in complete darkness before. I wouldn't be surprised if I end up fondling your ear or trying to make love to your belly button.'

'You're not doing too badly so far.'

'Thanks for the compliment,' he said, dryly. 'I'm going to need to put the light on for a second, is that OK? I promise not to look at you.'

'Yes, that's fine,' Clover said, trying to suppress a laugh. He was trying so hard.

A few seconds later, Angel managed to find the switch for the bedside lamp and the whole room was flooded with light. Clover blinked a few times to get her eyes accustomed to it and so did Angel.

He turned his attention to the floor and then got down on his hands and knees, clearly to try to find the condom under the bed.

'Jesus, did the thing bounce?' Clover giggled, watching Angel stark naked as he fumbled around trying to find it.

'Apparently so,' Angel said and then held it up triumphantly.

Clover laughed.

He brushed his hair back from his face and she noticed he was deliberately not looking at her. He was being so respectful and she loved him a little bit for it.

'I've killed the mood, haven't I?' Angel said.

'Not at all.'

'My ineptitude hasn't put you off?'

'It's made me want you even more.'

He grinned. 'I'll get the light.'

She reached out a hand to stop him. 'Leave it for a moment, come back up here.'

He climbed back on the bed. Lying down next to her, he stroked her arm, his eyes filled with warmth for her. She stared at him, their noses almost touching as she stroked his face. This man filled her up. Why had she ever been scared of being intimate with him? He was the most wonderful man she'd ever met.

'If you want to stop, we don't have to do this,' Angel said, gently.

She swallowed and shook her head. 'I want you so much.'

'I want you too, but—'

She placed her fingers on his lips. 'No buts, let's do this.'

'OK, shall I turn off the light?'

She nodded.

He kissed her briefly before pulling back slightly, his eyes filled with complete adoration as he gazed at her as if trying to commit her to memory, then he leaned over and switched off the light and immediately that connection was gone.

He kissed her, rolling over on top of her, caressing her, but all of a sudden this felt all wrong.

He shifted back slightly and then she heard him rip open

the condom wrapper. He gently moved her legs, settling himself between them. But it didn't matter how gentle he was being, this wasn't right. She didn't want to make love to him like this. This was just sex and there was more between them than that.

'Wait, stop. Put the light back on,' Clover said.

Angel immediately reached over and switched the lamp back on, his eyes registering concern as soon as light filled the room.

'Are you OK?'

'Yes, I just... I want to see your eyes when we make love.'

His face cleared, a smile appearing on his lips, and she felt her body relax again at the warmth and tenderness she saw there. This was how they were supposed to be together. She knew that this wasn't forever, for either of them, but she needed this connection. She wrapped her arms and legs around him, holding him close as he slid carefully inside her.

He stayed there, not moving, for the longest time, just staring down at her with complete adoration.

'Hey,' he said, softly, almost as if seeing her for the first time.

She stroked his face. 'Hi.'

He bent his head and kissed her softly and ever so slowly started moving against her, his breath heavy against her lips, that feeling building inside her almost immediately.

He pulled back slightly to look at her, his tender gaze filling her right up.

God, this was exactly what she needed. Whenever she thought about sex in the future, she would remember this, Angel's body against hers, his kiss, his touch. She stared up at him, swallowing the lump of emotion as she realised this was so much more than that. She would remember how they'd fitted together perfectly, the way he'd looked at her as if she was the only woman in the world, almost as if... he loved her. She'd remember how her heart had felt full, how he'd taken care of her, how he'd made her feel.

She reached up to stroke his cheek and trailed her thumb across his lips. He kissed it, then kissed her palm and her wrist, his eyes locked with hers the whole time.

He paused for a moment, staring at her. 'God, Clover, I've wanted this with you for so long and now we're here... I just... I wasn't expecting this.'

Did he feel this connection too?

He kissed her as he started moving again, but she could tell he was holding back. His touch was so gentle, his movements so careful, everything he was doing was for her and it brought tears to her eyes. She'd always had passionate, fast, hard sex before. It had never been like this. This was infinitely better, more tender, more... loving. That feeling was building inside her with every touch and as she moaned and trembled in his arms she felt like she was floating, taking Angel with her, enveloped in pure bliss. She felt him fall apart too, but he was still gentle as he fell over the edge, taking his time as he held her close.

He pulled back to look at her, their hearts pounding together, their breath heavy. There were no words, they just stared at each other.

She knew when she looked back at this moment it would be because she'd just had the most incredible sex in her entire life.

CHAPTER SEVENTEEN

Angel woke in the early hours of Thursday morning to find Clover lying in his arms, her head on his chest.

God, the night before had been magnificent. He'd had sex with quite a few women in his life but he hadn't experienced anything like that. He'd thought that sex with Clover would be great, they had a connection, but he hadn't expected it to be quite so wonderful as it was, and he had no idea why it was so different.

One thing was for sure though, he wasn't ready to walk away from it just yet. Clover had made it clear that she just wanted one night, that this wasn't a commitment for either of them, and that had suited Angel just fine but now he was wondering how he could prolong it for a little bit longer.

Except he was supposed to be leaving. In a little over forty-eight hours he'd be gone. That wasn't enough time.

She stirred in his arms and he felt her stretch along the length of him, the warmth of her body against him a glorious feeling. She looked up at him sleepily and smiled when she saw he was awake.

Before she could get up, before the happy little bubble surrounding them could burst, before she could thank him for a great night and move on, he kissed her and she immediately responded. That was a good sign.

He pulled back slightly to look at her, stroking her back. 'How are you feeling?'

A huge smile spread across her face which at least partly answered his question. 'Last night was… perfect in every way. I only wish I'd been brave enough to take that step with you six months ago.'

'You weren't ready and that's OK. We had to get to know each other for you to trust me. I think we were better off because of it. I don't think it would have been as amazing as it was if we'd jumped into bed with each other after the first week.'

'No, probably not.'

'You were definitely worth the wait,' Angel said.

'Well I think the memory of my ex has been well and truly expunged.'

'I've been thinking about that.'

She slid her hand round the back of his neck, playing with his hair. 'You have?'

'I think if you are truly to eradicate the memory of Marcus, then I think we should probably have sex a few more times, just to be sure.'

She grinned. 'Is that right?'

'Yes, definitely.'

She sighed theatrically as if it was a hardship and he couldn't help smiling. 'I think you're probably right. I think we need to try out some different positions too, just to be thoroughly sure.'

He straightened his face and nodded as if he was taking this conversation very seriously. 'That's a very good idea.'

'If a job's worth doing...' she teased.

'Exactly.'

Her hand played across his chest and then beneath the sheets across his stomach. 'Do you have more condoms?'

'I have a whole bag.'

Clover laughed. 'You better go and get them then.'

He grinned and gave her a brief kiss then quickly clambered out of her bed and ran as fast as he could into his room. He found the bag inside his wardrobe – he hadn't wanted Clover to see them and feel any pressure to follow through with her fifth-date plans, so he'd hidden them away. He dug out a box and grabbed a few. He turned back to find Clover, standing in his doorway watching him, completely naked.

God she was an incredible sight. He'd not had a proper chance to enjoy her body the night before, having spent most of their time together in complete darkness. Although he had enjoyed exploring her with his hands and mouth, now he could enjoy her with his eyes too.

She moved towards him and pushed him down so he was sitting on the edge of the bed and without any preamble she straddled him, kissing him deeply.

God, he loved this new confident side of her and he loved that he had given that to her, that she trusted him enough to let that wall she'd built around her come tumbling down. He stroked his hands down her back, over her shoulders. He moved his mouth to her neck, her chest and then kissed her across her breast, taking her nipple into his mouth.

She let out a cry of pleasure which made his stomach clench with need. He eased her back slightly so he could put on a condom. She knelt up and, with his hands on her hips, he guided her down on top of him.

She let out a heavy sigh, as if she was relaxing into a hot

bath, as if he was the one thing she needed to make her feel good. That made his chest ache.

Clover leaned forward and kissed him and he moved his hands to her hair, cupping the back of her head as she started moving against him, slow, deep rolls of her hips that drove him to the point of insanity. Sex had never been like this before, this desperate need for someone. He stroked his hands down her back, kissing her neck and her shoulder so he could take a breath, steady himself. She clung onto his shoulders, soft little moans of pleasure falling from her mouth, which made him wild with desire.

He looked up at her, her eyes clouded with lust and need. He stroked across her breasts, teasing her with his thumbs, and he felt her breath hitch. He slid his hands down to her hips, holding her against him tighter, moving inside her harder. She kissed him, greedily, gasps of desire escaping her lips as he pushed her to the very edge. And then she was falling apart in his hands, moaning loudly against his lips, her body shuddering, her breath heavy, and he let go too, his need for her thundering through him like a waterfall.

Clover leaned her forehead against his, trying to catch her breath as he struggled to breathe himself. They stayed wrapped around each other for the longest time, just staring at each other, their connection so strong it was almost a tangible thing between them.

'Angel,' she whispered.

His name on her lips when the breath was still heavy from the pleasure he had given her was like a song.

'Clover…' he peppered soft kisses over her shoulder.

'That was nice,' Clover said.

He stilled with his mouth against her skin. Nice? The best sex of his entire life and she thought it was nice?

He pulled back to look at her and saw the mischief in her eyes, the smile playing on her lips.

'Nice, eh?'

She shrugged. 'I think you can do better. With a bit of practice.'

Clover climbed off him and sauntered off in the direction of the bathroom, giving him a seductive smile over her shoulder as she left the room.

He let out a bark of laughter and then chased after her. She let out a shriek of laughter as he caught up with her as she was getting in the shower.

He kissed her neck. 'I'm up for the challenge.'

CHAPTER EIGHTEEN

Clover pushed open the door to Cones at the Cove and saw that Skye and Aria were already in there helping themselves to breakfast. The café wasn't officially open for breakfast as people generally didn't want ice cream and dessert that early in the day, but now and again the sisters would meet there before it opened and they tried to do it more often now Jesse was here as he made the best pancakes. Served with some of the fresh fruit, it was a great start to the day. Usually it was an unwritten rule that it was girls only; Jesse was allowed as long as he stayed in the kitchen.

'What's this, no pancakes?' Clover said in alarm when she saw the bowls of chopped fruit but no chunky pancakes.

'Jesse's just making them, but he has made waffles which you might want to try instead,' Skye said, pushing the stack of fluffy waffles in Clover's direction. 'Trust me, they're amazing.'

Aria nodded her approval. 'I've just had a bite, they might even be better than the pancakes. And we're going to need filling up ready for the zombie run this afternoon.'

Clover took one and loaded it up with fresh fruit, then they all went to sit in their favourite booth with views over Emerald Cove.

Clover took a bite of the lauded waffle and moaned with appreciation. 'This really is good, Jesse has been holding out on us.'

'I know, I keep telling him he needs to move here so we can have his wonderful food every day,' Skye said, digging into her own waffle.

Clover exchanged a sad glance with Aria. That would make Skye's dreams come true. But she didn't think Jesse would ever do that; there was his daughter, Bea, to think of too so it wasn't that straightforward. Plus the fact that both of them refused to acknowledge they had feelings for each other added to the complications.

Skye looked up and saw the looks passing between Clover and Aria and shook her head. 'Look, we're happy with this arrangement. He comes here, I go there, we have no-strings-attached amazing sex and that's it. I know it's not conventional but in this day and age there are no conventional relationships anymore, everyone just does what works for them. And this works for us.'

Clover held up her hands apologetically. 'If you're happy, then we're happy.'

It was the same argument every time that Clover and Aria brought it up, so they had stopped talking about it now. Skye was right: this worked for them, who was Clover to judge?

'How's it going with Angel anyway?' Skye asked. 'Any amazing no-strings-attached sex for you yet?'

Clover blushed.

'Oh my god you have, haven't you,' Skye said, her eyes lighting up with excitement.

Clover nodded and smiled.

'And, how was it?' Aria said. 'I don't mean specifics but, how did you find it, were you scared?'

'No, not one bit. I've never had sex before where the other person cared so much. I mean it's sex, right, it's fun and exciting and it feels good. But this felt so different.'

'It wasn't good?' Skye said.

'God, yes. it was perfect in every way. Every touch was about me, what I wanted and needed. The first time we made love he was so patient and gentle and considerate with me I honestly couldn't have hoped for anything more.'

'The first time? How many times were there?' Skye said, obviously needing a lot more details than Aria.

Clover smiled. 'Including just before I came here, four.'

Skye clapped her hands together with undisguised glee, letting out a squeal loud enough that Jesse poked his head out the kitchen to see if everything was OK.

Skye waved him away. 'We're just talking about sex, dear, nothing to worry about.'

Jesse rolled his eyes affectionately and ducked his head back inside.

'I'm so glad you had such a wonderful experience with Angel,' Aria said. 'I know the thought of having sex again was hanging over you like a dark cloud. And how is everything else going with him?'

Clover nodded, focussing her attention on impaling some strawberries on her fork. She cleared her throat. 'Good.'

She spotted the worried looks between Aria and Skye.

Clover sighed. 'He's leaving, on Saturday. That's two days.'

'Oh god. Noah's offered him a new job, hasn't he?' Aria said.

Clover nodded. 'Noah's old job actually. He'll be in charge of all the renovations, the new staff, building the hotels back up and selling them on.'

'Yes, I talked about this with Noah, how Angel would get bored with staying put, but I didn't realise he'd be leaving so soon,' Aria said.

'It just feels like we've barely started and now he's going. I don't feel we'll have the chance to see what will happen between us.'

'I thought you weren't interested in anything more than casual; you weren't looking for a serious relationship?' Skye said.

Clover shook her head. 'I wasn't, I'm not. I don't know, I just feel I'm not ready for this to be over yet.'

'It doesn't have to be over just because he's leaving,' Aria said.

'He'll be gone for a month, maybe more while he tries to find a hotel he wants to work with. And I don't think either of us signed up for a long-distance relationship.' Clover popped a strawberry into her mouth as she thought. 'Maybe this is for the best. If I'd spent weeks or months dating Angel, I think I could very easily fall in love with him and I don't want that.'

'Why don't you want that?' Aria said, gently.

'Because when you're in love, it hurts so much more when they betray you.'

Aria and Skye stared at her in shock and she wished she could take those words back.

'I never realised you were in love with Marcus,' Skye said, after a while.

'I wasn't, of course not, the man was vile, I couldn't possibly love someone like that,' Clover said, knowing it was a complete lie.

'But he wasn't vile in the beginning, we all thought he was great,' Aria said.

'I didn't,' Skye said. 'There was something about him that

gave me the creeps. I never said anything because you thought the world of him, but I didn't like him.'

'Well, I wish you had said something now,' Clover muttered.

'Would it have made a difference?'

'It might have turned on my radar, as it was it was well and truly malfunctioning when I met Marcus.'

'That's not your fault though,' Aria said. 'Everyone thought he was wonderful, it was a big shock to everyone when we found out what he'd done to you and those other women.'

Clover nodded. Even all of his friends had been sickened by what Marcus had done.

'No matter what happens between you and Angel, he is never going to betray you like that,' Skye said.

'I know,' Clover said, quietly. 'It's just putting my trust in him is a lot harder than I thought. I realise now that dating, kissing and sex, I was never really fearful of any of those things, and Angel has made all of that so easy. It was trusting someone enough to want forever that I'm scared of. I have dated a lot of men over the years, I never once thought about forever until I met Marcus. What he did humiliated me of course, I was angry and hurt, but it hurt all the more because I loved and trusted this man. He was my world. And not only did he betray me in the worst possible way but he destroyed my hopes and dreams for a future too. And every time I think about a possible future with Angel I remember I had those thoughts with Marcus and it scares me.'

Skye and Aria stared at her and she hated she'd brought the mood down.

'Oh, this is all pointless anyway. Angel is leaving and he's already said that he has no intention of settling down, he wants to travel the world. This job is an amazing opportunity for him. I don't want to get in the way of that. As I said, maybe it's for the best. I'm clearly not ready for that kind of relationship.' Clover looked between her sisters. 'Can we just talk about something else?'

Skye looked like she wanted to say something more.

'Please,' Clover said. 'I'm so embarrassed that I fell for Marcus in the first place, that I could have feelings for someone so disgusting, that I'd quite like to forget all about it.'

'OK,' Skye said. 'I'll say no more.'

'I have some news,' Aria said, clearly trying to defuse the tension. Clover turned to her eagerly. 'Me and Noah have been approved for adoption.'

'Oh my god, that's fantastic news,' Clover said.

'I'm so happy for you,' Skye said.

'We're both delighted,' Aria said.

'So what happens now?' Skye asked.

'We've said we'd like an older child, maybe around the age of five, so now they have to find one they think might be suitable for us. That could take days or weeks or months. Once they have a match for us, then we'll get to meet them, spend some time with them before they come to live with us. It's still a long road ahead of us but at least the biggest hurdle is behind us.'

Clover reached across the table to hold her sister's hand. 'You're going to make an amazing mum.'

'Thank you and you two get to be aunties and spoil the kid rotten.'

Clover exchanged smiles with her twin. 'We can't wait.'

Aria's life was complete, she had a hotel that was thriving, a man she loved, she was most likely getting engaged the next day and soon they'd be parents. It was hard not to want that, even if Clover couldn't imagine ever having it.

~

Angel sat down opposite Noah who was staring out the window overlooking Pearl Beach, with a big smile on his face, his coffee going cold in front of him.

'What are you looking so happy about?' Angel said, as one of the waitresses came over to take his order. He ordered a coffee and a bacon sandwich and turned his attention back to his friend.

Noah took a sip of his coffee, the smile still on his face. 'I know you're going to give me hell about this, but I don't even care. I was just thinking how much my life has changed in the last six months, how completely and utterly happy I am with Aria.'

'I'm not going to give you hell. I'm happy for you, truly I am.'

Noah grinned. 'I'm going to propose.'

'Really?'

Noah nodded. 'I should have done it months ago. I was just wary of rushing into it like I did with my last marriage, but I've always known Aria was my forever.'

'You two are made for each other,' Angel said. 'When are you going to do it?'

'Friday night, I think, during the lantern walk through the gardens.'

'Well if you need any help putting it together, you know where I am.'

'Thanks. I might get you to video it actually – if you're not doing anything tomorrow night and if you can do it discreetly and not get in the way.'

'I'm good at staying out the way.'

The waitress returned with Angel's and Noah's food and for a while they were silent as they tucked into their breakfasts.

'You don't want that for yourself one day?' Noah said, in between mouthfuls of food.

Angel took a swig of his coffee. 'You know, if you had asked me that a few months ago, my answer would have been an emphatic no. But now... I'm starting to think about things differently.'

'Because of Clover?' Noah asked, dipping his toast into his runny egg.

Angel took a big bite of his sandwich so he would have time to think about his reply. 'I'm not ready to settle down yet but eventually I'd like what you have. I'd like to fall in love and make a family,' he answered, carefully.

'And what happens if you fall in love before you're ready to settle down?'

'I've never been in love before. I've never met anyone who has ever tempted me to give up travelling the world. It would have to be someone incredible.'

Someone like Clover.

He immediately pushed that thought away. But no matter how hard he tried to deny it, he knew things could get very serious with Clover if he let it. Hell, it already felt like things were going that way and it had only been three dates. It wasn't love, he was pretty sure about that, but he had never felt this way before about anyone.

'You are one of the most open-minded people I know,' Noah said. 'We've eaten at restaurants all over the world and you have tried every food available from brains and cockroaches to some of the weirdest-looking fruits. You've been on terrifying rollercoasters and had crazy exhilarating experiences. It wouldn't hurt to keep an open mind about love too. Of all the things you will experience in life, love will be the greatest.'

Angel stared at him. 'Bloody hell. Are you going to be

running round the island singing "The Hills Are Alive"? I'm happy you've found Aria and your life has changed for the better, but I'm not sure I like this... *flowery* version of you. I liked it better when you were insulting me.'

Noah laughed. 'Fine, asshat. Here endeth the lesson. I'm just saying if you want to stay here and not go to Rome, I'm totally fine with that.'

Angel had woken up this morning with Clover's naked body entwined with his own and he had thought about asking Noah if he could put off going to Rome for a few more weeks. But what would happen after that? Would he want to stay here for a few more weeks and a few more? Being with Clover was addictive and he didn't want it to end anytime soon. But he didn't feel like he could put his whole life on hold for a casual relationship. Clover had said many times that she was only interested in something fun. She'd also referred to the time they'd spent together as not real dates, implying that they were just playing at dating. It didn't exactly fill him with hope if he did decide to stay.

He cleared his throat. 'No, I'm really looking forward to the opportunity.'

That was true. It would take something amazing to make him want to walk away from that.

'Well if that's the case, there's another hotel I'd like you to take a look at after you've been to Rome. This one is in Sydney. You could spend two weeks in Italy and then fly out to Australia and spend a few weeks there. Then you can decide which hotel you'd like to work on. I may even find another one for you after that.'

He'd be away from Clover for a month or more and although he'd known that had been a possibility, now it was real. He tried to ignore the pain he felt in his chest at that thought.

'That's fine. I love Australia.'

'I know you do.'

Clover had always wanted to go to Australia, maybe she would want to come with him. Or maybe it would be better to have a clean break between them before things got messy and complicated. Walk away and move on.

That was going to be a lot harder than he thought.

CHAPTER NINETEEN

'Remind me again why we're doing this?' Skye grumbled as she did some cursory stretches.

'Because when I told all the islanders they had to get involved with every aspect of the Halloween fair, that means us as well,' Aria said.

Clover smiled, exchanging looks with Skye. They adored their elder sister, and Clover knew that Skye would bend over backwards to make Aria happy, but that didn't mean she would be happy about it, especially when, as in today's activity, it involved a lot of running.

'It will be fun and I thought it would suit your competitive streak,' Aria said. 'If you're one of the first ten to make it across the finish line, you'll win a trophy.'

Skye didn't exactly look thrilled about that.

'And one of Jesse's cupcakes,' Aria said.

'Ah well, now you're talking. If I'd known they were waiting for me at the finish line, I'd have started the race by now. Where are the boys anyway? Surely if we have to suffer, they do too.'

Clover looked around. Where was Angel? He'd said he wanted to film this. But she also knew he wanted to research about the hotel in Italy before he went at the weekend so maybe he was still busy doing that.

'Oh, they're all doing something else for me,' Aria said, vaguely.

She was always good at finding jobs for people. Clover couldn't help but be a bit disappointed that she wasn't going to do this with Angel.

'So what are the rules?' Clover asked. 'Or is it relatively straightforward?'

'Basically, there are twelve obstacles we have to get over or under and then a race to the finish line,' Aria shrugged, as if it was as simple as that.

'And not forgetting we have to avoid getting attacked by zombies along the way,' Clover said.

'Oh yes, there is that,' Aria grinned.

'What happens when the zombies catch us, are we allowed to lamp them?' Skye asked and Clover laughed. She laughed even louder when Aria's face fell.

'No, of course not. We do not want to get sued because one of the *actors* gets a broken nose.'

'So they can maul us, but we can't maul them?' Skye asked, clearly trying to wind Aria up.

'There will be no mauling, by anyone, it's supposed to be relatively non-contact. Every participant has these three flags attached to their belt,' Aria said, indicating the tags hanging off her back. 'The zombies will be going for them, not for you.'

'Skye's just trying to wind you up,' Clover said. 'She's not going to punch anyone.'

'Where's the fun in that?' Skye said and then held her hands up when Aria shot her a glare. 'OK, OK, I promise, I won't punch anyone.'

The voice of Seamus, the mayor, came over the loud-speaker, welcoming everyone to the zombie run, explaining the rules and reiterating several times that the zombies were not allowed to be attacked.

There was a countdown and then they were off. For a few minutes there was a bit of a bottleneck as all the villagers and hotel guests tried to squeeze through the starting posts and then everyone was running flat out along Diamond Sands for the first obstacle. Up ahead, Clover could see zombies were waiting for the runners, some pouring out of the caves along the beach, some lurking near the obstacles. The runners were shrieking with delight or terror as they started to be chased. Even as Clover was running to the first obstacle, she could see the zombies were made up really well. Whoever had been in charge of make-up and costumes had done a fabulous job: skin was hanging off, there were cuts, bruises and blood everywhere, it was horribly gory, which the children especially were absolutely loving. She could see some of the adults were more terrified than having fun, but she supposed that it was the same kind of terror you felt when watching a great horror film, although she'd never really been into them herself.

She launched herself at the first obstacle, which was a small inflatable climbing wall with a slide at the other side. Sure enough, the zombies were there waiting at the end of the slide. One reached out to grab her and she dodged away with a shriek. Skye laughed next to her as she ducked under the waiting arms of another zombie.

They raced on, Clover inching ahead. She checked over her shoulder to see that Aria and Skye were still close behind, Aria with a look of determination, Skye clearly having the time of her life, despite the earlier protests.

They reached the next obstacle, an inflatable castle with

several doors they had to squeeze through. There were a few screams of terror from the runners as there were clearly zombies waiting for them on the other side. Clover pushed her way through the wall and saw several zombie hands reach out to grab at her. She ducked, dived, dodged her way through and when she'd made it through the throng was quite surprised that she still had her three flags intact.

Up ahead, a tall zombie wearing a ripped and bloody shirt that clung to large muscles was waiting with outstretched arms for her. Large parts of his face was hanging off and the rest of his face made him look like he'd been clawed to death by a giant werewolf. She'd never gone in for gore and now that this was right in front of her, approaching her threateningly, it made her like it even less.

She feinted to the left, and then ran to the right, dodging past him with ease. As she ran on to the next obstacle, the zombie was still in hot pursuit, but it seemed she was faster than he was. She was sure he would give up soon.

The next obstacle was a large inflatable forest and she could see the runners, squeezing their way in between the inflatable trees. She hoped there weren't zombies lurking in there. She started pushing her way through, but as she looked over her shoulder the tall zombie was still close behind.

She made it to the other side and carried on running but the zombie was still chasing her. Up ahead, she saw a zombie that looked suspiciously like Jesse – he was such a huge, distinctive man that he was clearly recognisable, even with all his make-up. Skye let out a bark of a laugh as she spotted Jesse too.

Nearby, there was another zombie and Clover thought he looked like Noah. If they were here as zombies, then Angel was here too. Suddenly, she realised who was chasing her and she stopped dead, turning to face her attacker.

The zombie slowed and stopped a few metres away and, through all the make-up, she immediately recognised Angel's beautiful blue eyes. She saw him smile as he realised she knew who he was and she couldn't help smiling too.

'You want me, you're going to have to catch me,' Clover said.

'Oh I intend to,' Angel said.

She turned and ran flat out for the next obstacle, a series of low inflatable tubes she had to climb over. She clambered over one successfully but stumbled before she reached the next. She managed to get up just as Angel was climbing over the first tube, but she'd lost precious seconds. She quickly climbed over the next three with Angel right behind her – at one point she even felt his fingers on her back.

As they ran towards the next obstacle they came to a narrow part of the beach where caves lined the cliffs. Clover knew these caves like the back of her hand, having spent hours exploring them as a child. There was a narrow one just up ahead and she knew that it actually joined one of the other caves further down. Maybe she could lose him in there.

She headed for the cave and slid through the crack which then opened out into a larger cavern. It was cool and dark in here and she waited a moment for her eyes to become accustomed to the darkness so she could find her way through. But those precious seconds cost her dearly as suddenly Angel was there with her, his chest heaving, a huge smile on his face.

'Now you're mine.'

Suddenly being caught by Angel didn't seem like a bad thing, after all.

She backed up against the wall as he approached, pressing her flags into the cave wall so he couldn't get them.

'What are you going to do with me?' Clover said, putting on her best damsel in distress voice.

Angel put his hands either side of her, leaning against the wall and caging her in.

'Well, zombies normally rip out the throats of their victims, so let's start with that.'

Angel kissed her throat softly, making all thoughts of running away or completing the course instantly fade away. He placed another kiss on the place where her neck met her shoulder and then trailed his hot mouth to just under her ear. Christ, this man.

He pulled back to look at her and she reached out to gently hold his face so she could have a proper look at him.

'This looks amazing.'

'Do you still fancy me like this?'

'I've never found a rotting corpse sexy, but I could totally get on board with this.'

'Necrophilia, bit weird, but OK, I won't judge you.'

She smiled. 'Where else would the zombie feast on me?'

'Ripping your throat out wasn't enough?'

She shook her head.

He studied her, his eyes assessing her for a moment. 'Zombies like eating hearts, when the heart is pounding furiously and filled with blood.'

'Is that right?'

He nodded, his eyes casting down to her chest. 'What do you have on under this top?'

'Why don't you find out?' Clover said.

She was wearing a thin zip-up hoodie, but nothing else underneath. She'd thought she might get warm doing the course but the day was quite cold.

Angel slowly unzipped her top and let out a heavy breath when he saw she was wearing only a bra.

'Well, that's a lovely surprise,' he said.

She wondered if he would take her bra off too, or touch

her breasts as he definitely seemed to like touching them when they had sex, but he dipped his head and placed a gentle kiss right above her heart.

Oh God. What was clearly supposed to be sexy, or even silly with all the zombie talk, suddenly felt so much more than that, it felt... romantic, loving. There was so much tenderness in this single kiss and it nearly brought tears to her eyes. God, how could he kiss her like this and then walk away in a few days' time? Did he not feel this thing between them? Was this really just casual for him?

She lifted his chin, studying his face for a moment, trying to read what was going on in his head, but she had no idea what he was thinking. She leaned up and kissed him, wrapping her hands round his neck, pressing herself around him as he held her tight in his arms. Kissing him was so much more than anything she'd ever experienced before, their connection so deep. His hands slipped beneath her top, caressing her bare back and making her tremble with need for him.

His hands moved lower and then she heard a strange ripping sound which she recognised a few seconds too late. She immediately stepped back and saw Angel was holding one of her flags triumphantly in the air.

She let out a laugh. 'You arse, you tricked me.'

'It didn't seem you were putting up too much of a fight,' he said. 'I know they said that the runners weren't allowed to attack the zombies but I didn't think you would give it to me that willingly.'

She tried to swipe it from his hands and he held it out of reach. She couldn't help but laugh at his underhanded tactics.

'Right, I better go, I have more runners to catch,' Angel said, adding the flag to a small stash he had at his belt.

'Hopefully not in the same way you caught me,' Clover said.

Angel looked up, all humour now gone from his face.

They had never spoken about this arrangement being exclusive, but she'd always assumed it was. It wasn't as if he had the opportunity to sleep around with lots of other women while he was here, he was always busy during the day and they'd spent almost every night since his return sharing a bed. They hadn't needed to make rules for this before, and it was going to be over shortly anyway. But, as ridiculous as it seemed, Clover suddenly wanted that reassurance from him, regardless of whether he had the opportunity or not.

He walked back towards her and took her face in his hands. 'I would never, ever need someone else while I'm with you. My whole life, I've always wanted more, I had to climb the tallest skyscraper, go on the world's largest rollercoaster, and when I did these things, it never felt like it was enough. But you, you are enough for me. My cup has always been half full, but you fill me up to the top.'

She stared at him, stunned by this raw, beautiful honesty.

She leaned up and kissed him again and he held her tight. She pulled back slightly. 'You fill me up too,' she whispered. 'So I'm overflowing.'

He stared at her, eye to eye, and he looked like he wanted to say something, but he didn't. He kissed her on the nose and then stepped back.

'I'll see you at the finish line.'

With that, he ran out of the cave and she was left trying to catch her breath. What he felt for her was way more than just friendship.

She quickly zipped up her top and ran out the cave. There were still a lot of runners doing the course but most of the participants had finished now. She raced through the remaining obstacles, avoiding zombies as much as she could, and ran across the finish line still with one flag remaining.

'Hey, what happened to you? We lost sight of you,' Skye said, behind her. Clover turned and Skye laughed. 'It looks like you have a bit of stage make-up around your face.'

Clover touched her face, realising that Angel must have left some of his make-up on her when they'd kissed. But she noticed that Skye and Aria both had make-up smudged round their faces too.

'So much for not mauling the zombies. Looks like you both had fun,' Clover said.

'Oh I certainly did,' Skye said. 'Are you OK, you look a bit... stunned.'

'No, I'm fine, just... you know, tired. That obstacle course was challenging.'

She would keep her thoughts to herself for now, but it felt like something had changed between her and Angel, if only she was brave enough to explore it.

Clover watched Angel over the table in her tiny kitchen, his face lit up by the flickering candles. They'd had a wonderful afternoon, making love, talking and laughing. And now she'd just finished a delicious candlelit meal he'd cooked for her. It couldn't have been more romantic.

'Why are you doing all this?' Clover said. 'You've already got me into bed, multiple times, and I can guarantee you, we'll be having sex again tonight. You don't need to pull out all the stops to impress me, I'm a done deal.'

Angel finished his glass of wine. 'This was never about sex for us, Clover. This was never about impressing you so I could get you into bed. Maybe in the beginning, when I first met you, I would have been happy with just that, but this is so much more than that now.'

She wanted to ask him how much more. She wanted to ask him to stay for a bit longer to see if this turned out to be as wonderful as she hoped it would be. But she did none of those things. There were so many reasons why she didn't feel like she could. Later, she would tell herself she didn't ask him to stay because he seemed so keen to leave, and she didn't want to hold him back from following his dreams, from taking a job he would love. She didn't want to guilt him in to staying, she didn't want him to feel obligated to her because of what they'd started and because he didn't want to hurt her. She wanted him to *want* to stay.

And all of those reasons were true but she knew in her heart the main reason she couldn't ask him to stay was because, if he did, things would no longer be casual between them. They'd be starting down a road that was a serious relationship and she just didn't feel ready for that.

'Come on, I have a surprise for you,' Angel said, getting up and grabbing her coat, before holding it out to her.

She stood up and slipped her coat on. 'Where are we going?'

'You'll see.'

She smiled and took his hand as they stepped outside. It was a cold night, but the sky was clear, thousands of stars sparkling from an inky canvas, the moon shining bright as it lit the way.

She presumed they were heading back to the hotel for some reason as they were heading that way but she was surprised when he veered off to go over the headland towards the village. She hoped they weren't going to take part in the Halloween activities. That would put an end to the romantic evening if they were being chased by a man with a chainsaw.

He stopped by the old oak tree and she suddenly noticed

the ladder, propped up against the trunk, leading up to the treehouse.

'Oh my god,' Clover said, her eyes lighting up with excitement.

'I'm not as clever as your dad when it comes to making a rope ladder on a pulley, but I'm sure we can fashion something. This will have to do for now.'

'Have you been up there?' Clover said, looking up the ladder to the little hatch above them.

'Yes.'

'What's it like? Oh god, was it a mess?'

'Why don't you go up and have a look.'

Clover tested the ladder and then started climbing up. She reached the hatch, flipped the catch and pushed it open. It was dark inside as she clambered up and she waited for her eyes to become accustomed to the darkness before moving across the floor slowly so that Angel could step up beside her. Her foot came in contact with something soft and she cringed, hoping to god it wasn't a dead animal.

Angel climbed up beside her.

'I think we need to come back in the daylight, I can't see a thing.'

'It's OK, I have that covered.'

He stepped away from her and a few seconds later hundreds of fairy lights lit up the room. She blinked a few times because it was exactly how she remembered it. The soft, bright red rug on the floor, the brightly coloured beanbags, the telescope, the radio, even a pile of books on one of the shelves.

'I don't understand. It's been nearly ten years since I've been up here, but it all looks brand new.'

'It is new, but I was able to see how it was when I first came up here, plus Aria showed me photos of it from when you were a kid. It wasn't too bad up here; your dad did a good job of keeping it all fairly watertight. But I replaced everything just in case of any damage or insects.'

'This is amazing,' Clover said, crossing over to the telescope and peering out at the village. It was all lit up with the Halloween festivities, people were moving around having fun. She could see the decorations and people dressed up. This telescope was far better than the one she'd had as a kid. She moved it over slightly to focus on the woods behind the village.

'I can see the pumpkins for tomorrow's Pumpkin Treasure Hunt. We might be able to get a head start by spotting them all now,' she laughed.

Behind her the radio came on and she turned to face Angel. 'I can't believe you'd do all this for me.'

'Why wouldn't I? I love... spending time with you and making you smile.'

'This is wonderful. I have so many fond memories of this place, of being here with my dad, of hanging out with my friends. Thank you for giving this back to me.'

'It's my absolute pleasure, but it wasn't entirely altruistic. I thought as I can't come to the ball with you, I thought you might want to dance with me tonight instead.'

She smiled. 'I would love to.'

He wrapped his arms around her and she looped her arms round his neck and they started moving slowly round the treehouse.

'I'm sure, as a dance teacher, this kind of shuffling instead of proper dancing makes you cringe, but it's the best I can do. Unless you want to see more of my amazing ballet?' Angel said.

She smiled as she looked up at him. 'This is perfect.'

He bent his head and kissed her briefly. She leaned her

head against his chest, listening to his heart as they swung around the room.

She closed her eyes, shutting out the world so it was just the two of them. If she tried really hard, she could pretend that he wasn't leaving in two days after all.

CHAPTER TWENTY

Clover hurried down to the village the next day, pulling her hair up into a ponytail as she followed the path over the headland. The village was still thriving, despite the fact that it was Friday and the fair had been running for the last week. She'd have thought that the children and families who were staying at the hotel would have got bored with the fair by now, but it was still as busy as it had been on the first day. Although she knew that a lot of day trippers were coming to the island from local areas to experience the fair for themselves, so maybe some of the people here were from nearby towns and villages rather than hotel guests.

Today was the day of the Great Pumpkin Treasure Hunt and she and her sisters had been badgered into being part of the hotel team. All the local businesses were taking part, as well as the families and couples who were staying at the hotel, and there were prizes being handed out for the team that could find all the pumpkins the fastest. It sounded like a fun way to spend a few hours but mostly she was looking forward to spending some more time with Angel. They were going to be in a group with her sisters, Jesse and Noah but she was hoping she could lag behind with Angel. He was leaving in less than twenty-four hours and she wanted to make the most of the time they had left.

She was surprised when she reached the start of the treasure hunt to see that only Noah and Jesse were waiting for her. She knew she was a little late as her dance class had only just finished, but she'd have thought her sisters would have been here by now. And where was Angel? She hoped he hadn't forgotten.

'Hey,' Clover said as she approached. 'Where are the others?'

'Gone on ahead, they were eager to start,' Jesse said, awkwardly.

Clover narrowed her eyes. 'Aria, Skye and Angel?'

'Yes, um, they've taken the left path and we're going to take the right and we'll meet up in the middle and swap around then. This way both sides will get covered twice and we'll be less likely to miss any pumpkins,' Noah explained practically, as if it made total sense and there was no other reason.

'Angel wanted to wait for you but…' Jesse trailed off.

'My sisters bullied him into going with them?' Clover said.

'Something like that,' Noah muttered.

Clover groaned inwardly. There was no coincidence that this had happened after her chat with her sisters the day before. She wouldn't be surprised if they were giving him a hard time about leaving. Christ. She never would have said anything if she'd known that her sisters were going to be assholes about it.

'Come on then,' Clover said, sadly.

'Hey,' Noah nudged her gently. 'Whatever they want to say to him, it's not going to change his mind about you. He's crazy about you.'

'He said that?'

'Trust me. I've never seen him like this about any other woman before.'

'Oh, we're just good friends and yes we're sort of dating but I don't think it means anything. Not like that.'

'Well I'm not sure the just-good-friends thing is working out too well.'

'What do you mean?'

'Well it always gets slightly awkward when one person feels more than the other,' Noah said.

Clover cringed with embarrassment. Was it obvious to Angel that her feelings had changed?

'Tell me about it,' Jesse muttered as they made their way along the trail.

'Oh Jesse, Skye absolutely adores you. You know that. I have no idea why you two aren't happily married with hundreds of babies by now.'

'It's not as straightforward as you make it sound.'

'Pumpkin,' Noah said, pointing to one half hidden amongst the trees. This one was decorated like a cat.

Clover bent down to retrieve the number from the back and made a note of it on the clipboard.

They carried on down the path for a while.

'Are you staying here for the ball, Jesse, or will you be leaving us before then?' Clover asked, deciding to change the subject.

'I wouldn't miss it,' Jesse said. 'Will you be going with Angel?'

'No sadly, he'll be gone by then.'

'Ah, sorry about that,' Noah said. 'I do feel bad about offering him this job. Maybe I could have picked a better time.'

'Don't feel bad. You're giving him exactly what he wants, I can't be mad at you for that. You're making his dreams come true, just like you did for me, Skye and Aria. I just wish we had a little more time together, that's all.'

'How long will he be gone?' Jesse asked.

'Probably four to six weeks, initially, but once the sale goes through, I think he'll be gone for three or four months at a time, maybe longer,' Noah said.

Clover found another pumpkin and made a note of the number, trying to ignore the ache in her chest at the thought that she wouldn't see Angel for weeks, even months at a time.

There was a large pumpkin sculpture up ahead, several pumpkins balanced together and carved to look like a great dragon. Noah rushed ahead to take a photo of it, no doubt for the website.

'A bit of advice,' Jesse said to Clover, softly. 'From one member of the friends-with-benefits club to another, tell Angel how you feel before he leaves. You'll always regret it if you don't.'

Clover sighed. She was fairly sure her bloody sisters were doing that for her.

Angel took a photo of a pumpkin carved like Darth Vader, the golden light of the flickering candle gleaming from the eyes and mouth.

'This will look great on the website,' he said, hoping he could keep Skye and Aria distracted for long enough so they wouldn't get on to the topic of him and Clover, which was clearly what they wanted to talk about. They certainly hadn't dragged him off because they enjoyed his company.

'What are we going to do without you when you leave?' Aria said as they continued down the trail.

'I'll still be doing all this stuff for you, updating the

websites and doing your adverts and making video trailers and all that, but I'll be doing it while I'm in Italy or Australia or wherever I am in the world. You can't get rid of me that easily.'

'Yes, but all the little things you do so well, we're definitely going to miss you,' Aria said.

'I'll be back every few months.'

'It won't be the same as having you here all the time.'

It wouldn't be the same. Waking up with Clover wrapped in his arms every morning, he was definitely going to miss that.

'And look at this view,' Aria pointed out over Diamond Sands and beyond that to Emerald Cove, Sapphire Bay and Pearl Beach, stretching out along the length of Jewel Island. 'Surely you're not going to get better than this anywhere else in the world.'

'Jewel Island is a beautiful place,' Angel agreed. 'But there are many beautiful places in the world that I'd like to see.'

He glanced at Skye. She was yet to say anything and he wondered what was going on. At the moment their only ploy seemed to be to get him to stay, but he wasn't sure why.

'Won't you miss this place at all?' Aria went on. 'The community spirit, the villagers, the beaches... your friends.'

Lovely as it was, there was only one thing he would really miss about this place and that was Clover. God, the thought of not seeing her every day really hurt and he wasn't sure how he would get over that.

'I know this is your home and you're happy here, settled,' Angel said. 'Making a life for yourself here, raising a family one day, was your dream but settling down was never mine. I want to travel and see it all.'

'Don't you think dreams can change?' Skye said, breaking her silence.

Angel took a photo of another pumpkin carved like a big castle.

'Of course dreams can change, people change, but I don't think I have yet.'

'Well if that's your dream, who are we to stand in your way?' Skye said, sniffly, sounding like she'd very much like to stand in his way.

'I have to say that I didn't realise that me leaving would upset you both so much, I'm touched,' Angel said. He didn't feel remotely touched but he wasn't really sure what was going on.

'Well, before you go tomorrow, I'd like to say thanks,' Skye said and for a moment there wasn't a trace of her normal sarcasm. She saw his look of surprise. 'Genuinely. You've made Clover so happy and I haven't seen that for a long time. She was so scared about getting involved with a man again, putting her trust in someone, dating, having sex. And you have been so good for her, your patience and kindness has been the balm she never knew she needed. So truly, thank you from the bottom of my heart.'

Angel stared at her in surprise. 'Clover's my friend, I care about her too.'

Aria gave his arm a squeeze. 'I couldn't have asked for anyone better. You're perfect for her in every way.'

Suddenly it all made sense; they wanted him to stay for Clover. They had no idea this was something casual for her, that she wasn't interested in anything more serious or long-term.

'And what's lovely is she can finally move on,' Skye said. 'You've fixed her. Now she can have a proper relationship with someone else, fall in love, get married, have a baby – hell, have several babies.'

His stomach turned at that thought. Of course he wanted

Clover to be happy, but the thought of anyone else making love to her, marrying her, raising a family with her, made him green with envy. He didn't want to fix her for someone else.

But he had to accept that. It was never going to be anything more than casual for her. Eventually, when he'd gone, she would move on with someone else, she would find someone she did want serious with and he had to let her go.

He just had to make the most of the time he had left with her. Which begged the reason why he was spending the afternoon with her sisters and not her.

'Excuse me, I have something I need to do,' Angel said.

He turned and walked back along the path.

'Angel, wait,' Aria said but he hurried on.

He made his way back to the start and then took the other path, hurrying on past a bunch of pumpkins carved like a large dragon, and then he saw her, walking ahead with Jesse and Noah.

'Clover!'

She turned and looked around.

He caught up to her as Noah and Jesse waited a little way ahead.

He cupped her face in his hands and kissed her. She kissed him too, her hands stroking his back.

She giggled against his lips and pulled back slightly. 'Are you OK? Did you miss me that much?'

'Yes, let's get out of here.'

She studied his face in concern and then nodded.

Clover waved goodbye to Noah and Jesse and took his hand, pulling him back along the track. Suddenly she stopped and walked purposefully off the path through the trees until they were completely secluded amongst the bushes and plants. Up ahead, he saw a wooden lodge and as they drew closer, he realised it was a bird hide.

Clover tugged him straight inside and closed the door, immediately taking his face in her hands and kissing him again.

She pulled back, leaning her forehead against his for a moment. 'I'm sorry for whatever my sisters said. They mean well, but I wish they'd keep their noses out of it.'

'They didn't say anything I didn't already know, some cold, hard truths, I guess. I just... I have one day left before I leave and I want to spend as much time as possible with you before I do.'

She stared at him as if he was a complicated puzzle she was trying to work out and then she nodded and kissed him again.

To his surprise and relief, she started undressing him. He shuffled her back against the wall, pulling her hoodie and t-shirt off in one go. He quickly took off her bra, filling his hands with her breasts, and she let out a soft moan. He released her hair from her ponytail, letting it tumble over her shoulders. The rest of their clothes came off very easily. He quickly grabbed a condom from his jeans pocket, stepped back slightly to deal with it and then lifted her. She wrapped herself around him and then he was inside her, pinning her to the wall.

The moan that fell from her lips was pure need, a desperate desire for him, for more. She clawed at his shoulders, her head falling back, and he placed kisses over her throat. She looked back at him, touching her fingers across his lips before kissing him again, her tongue sliding inside his mouth.

An urgency ripped through him and he moved against her faster and harder. She held him tighter and then she was falling apart around him, crying out his name, his own release thundering through him. She kissed him hard, catching his moans on her lips, her breath heavy, her body shaking as he held her there tight in his arms.

'God, I don't want to lose this,' Angel whispered against her lips.

'We can have great sex like this every day if you stayed,' she said, casually, as if that was the only reason she wanted him to stay.

His heart sank a little.

'I think I'd need more than just great sex to make me want to stay,' he said, meaningfully.

She smiled sadly. 'I get that. You said yourself that you'd only give up your life for someone incredible.'

He frowned and opened his mouth to speak but she kissed him.

'I'm going to miss you so much,' she whispered against his lips.

'Clover—'

'And we'll always be friends right?'

He let out a little sigh. Was this really just a friends-with-benefits arrangement for her? But he supposed having her in his life as a friend was better than not having her at all.

'Yes, of course.'

'Then I think you better take me back home, because I have a few more positions I need to tick off my list before you go.'

He smiled slightly. 'Well, that I can do.'

CHAPTER TWENTY-ONE

Clover walked into Cones at the Cove later that afternoon. It was quieter, just a few stragglers remaining from the lunchtime rush. Clover knew Skye would close the café soon so they had an hour or two's break before the evening crowd descended on them, especially with the upcoming lantern walk that night.

There was no sign of Skye or Jesse out the front so she pushed the door open to the kitchen. Skye was giggling as she tried to force-feed Jesse a spoonful of ice cream and he was laughing as he tried to fend her off.

'What crazy flavour has Skye come up with now that she is trying to foist on you?' Clover said.

Jesse laughed. 'This one is curry flavoured. It's a step too far for me.'

'For me too,' Clover said. 'No one wants that.'

'Au contraire. I put this out as flavour of the day this morning and the container was completely empty by this afternoon,' Skye said.

'Oh well, people like to try different things,' Clover said.

'I have a new flavour I'm trialling for Christmas too, want to try that?' Skye said.

'As long as it doesn't have curry in it, I'm game.'

Skye scooped some pale brown ice cream into a bowl, grabbed a spoon and ushered Clover out into the café, just as the last customer was leaving. Skye waved them off.

They sat down in one of the booths and Clover sniffed the ice cream suspiciously.

'It's not poison,' Skye said, indignantly.

'You just told me you have curry ice cream on the menu, excuse me for being a bit cautious.'

'You'll like this one,' her sister insisted.

Clover took a small spoonful and popped it in her mouth. 'Oh wow, what is this? It's fruity and sweet and... Oh, is it mince-pie flavour?'

'Yes it is,' Skye beamed. 'What do you think?'

'It's delicious. You definitely need to put this on the menu next month.'

'I will. I thought about serving it with a brandy cream or maybe a brandy sauce.'

'Fantastic idea.' Clover took another mouthful. 'Can you believe that Noah is going to propose tonight.'

'I know. Aria deserves this, I'm so happy for her,' Skye said.

'Everything is coming together for her. She just needs the adoption agency to find her a child now and she has everything she's ever wanted. It kind of makes you reflect on your own life, doesn't it?'

Skye nodded, glancing over at Jesse.

Clover took another mouthful of ice cream. 'So what did you talk to Angel about today?'

Skye gave a little smile. 'Well, judging by the speed he took off to go and talk to you, maybe it worked.'

Clover smiled and shook her head. 'What were you trying to do?'

'We were trying to get him to stay,' Skye said. 'We didn't tell him anything, we didn't repeat what you told us, we were just... upselling the benefits of staying on Jewel Island.'

'He won't stay for me. His travels mean too much to him for him to change the habit of a lifetime.'

Skye sighed and looked over at Jesse who was singing to himself as he restocked the toppings bar. The look she gave him was one of pure love.

The radio was playing over by the counter and it was unlikely he would hear them but Clover leaned forward anyway and kept her voice low.

'Is this more to do with your relationship with Jesse than about me and Angel?' Clover asked, softly.

'He leaves on Monday,' Skye said. 'And Christ I'm going to miss him.'

Clover looked between the two of them. 'Do you ever think about going back to Canada with him?'

'Every damn day,' Skye said and then turned her attention back to Clover. 'I love working here at our hotel, I love what we've done with the café, I love Jewel Island and, most of all, I love working alongside you and Aria every day. You two are so important to me. But I miss him and Bea so much. I just don't know what I'd be returning for if I did go back. Would it just be more of this, more casual friends-with-benefits arrangement? Because of Bea, that's all he's ever wanted. Sex, friendship, no strings attached. Even before our little marriage of convenience he made it clear that was what he wanted.'

'But it became more than that when you got married,' Clover said. 'We both know that.'

'It did, well I thought it did. We lived together, Bea was there. We felt like a proper family. I love that little girl so much. But we agreed a year until I could get my working visa to stay and, when that year was up, *he* started arranging the divorce and started suggesting it might be a good idea if I got my own place. He'd told Bea from the beginning that I was only staying for a year, that this wasn't forever, and he repeated that throughout our short-lived marriage until even Bea was asking when I was leaving. So I moved out and we still saw each other as friends and sometimes, when Bea wasn't around, friends with benefits and it killed me to go from... my dream to... so much less than that. I don't want to return to that. Separate houses, friends, occasional sex. This, what we have now, almost feels better than that, like a holiday romance four or five times a year when he comes here or I go there. But I see your friends-with-benefits arrangement with Angel and it worries me that you're going to end up down the same path. I worry you'll be waiting for him to come back from his travels, when you'll have a few weeks of great, casual sex before he bogs off around the world again, neither of you being prepared to take that step for something more, to tell each other how you feel. That's no way to live your life. I want more for you. Even if I can't have that, I wish for you to have so much more.'

Clover sighed. 'I don't know if I'm ready for more. I don't want him to leave, I'm loving having this time with him, but I have nothing to offer him either. It would be like you going back to Canada for casual sex with Jesse, I'd be asking Angel to give up his whole life, his dreams for no-strings-attached sex. And honestly I don't know whether he would stay even if I was offering him more than that. Look, as you said this morning, this works for us right now. We're both happy with this arrangement so why change it?'

She focussed her attention on her ice cream. Maybe if she kept telling herself that, she'd start to believe it.

~

Angel took Clover's hand as they left the hotel that evening. That night had been billed as a Halloween lantern walk and it had proved very popular with the hotel guests and locals. The gardens were all lit up with Halloween lights and decorations, glowing ghosts were hanging from the trees, and illuminated oversized pumpkins and various other characters were strewn across the grounds. It was supposed to be a much gentler, family-friendly night-time entertainment from that taking place in the village. There had been hundreds of people streaming through the gardens earlier in the evening but now it was much quieter, with only a few stragglers remaining. The atmosphere was more serene and tranquil now, than scary. The lights almost looked romantic.

He glanced down at Clover and she smiled up at him. His chest hurt. Less than twenty-four hours and he'd be gone, and what they had would be over. He wouldn't see her for a month or more and when he came back they'd probably be nothing more than friends.

'It's so pretty, isn't it,' Clover said.

He cleared his throat. 'It's lovely.'

'And a perfect night for a proposal, I don't think Aria has any idea. They've been so busy with this fair and going through all the paperwork for the adoption that I don't think a proposal has been on her radar. She knows what she has with Noah is forever and she knows that they will probably get married at some point, but she doesn't need that affirmation from him. Imagine being that secure in your relationship that you know your love will last a lifetime.'

'I honestly have no idea what that feels like,' Angel said.

'No, me neither,' Clover said, sadly.

He cringed, knowing that she had loved Marcus and he

had betrayed her in the worst possible way. It would be hard for her to ever put her trust in someone again. He wanted to show her that she could trust in love again but how could he do that when he was leaving the next day?

'What time is Noah going to do it?' Clover said.

Angel noticed the subject change and decided to let it drop. 'I have a motion-sensor camera rigged up so as soon as they arrive, the camera will come on and we'll get notified and we'll be able to watch it on my mobile.'

'Oh that's cool. Do you think they will mind us watching?'

'Noah didn't seem to have any problem with it. Obviously we haven't asked Aria but we all know how close you three are, you tell each other everything. So I doubt she would mind.'

Clover laughed. 'Not everything.'

'Did you tell them we'd had sex?'

She giggled. 'I might have mentioned it.'

Angel rolled his eyes but he didn't really mind. He loved his sisters but he'd never had that kind of closeness with them. It must be lovely to have that with someone, a sibling or a friend. He was close with Noah, but he wouldn't dream of sharing his sex life with him.

His phone suddenly beeped to tell him the camera had picked up motion.

'Here we go,' Angel said, fishing his phone from his pocket.

Clover squealed in excitement.

They quickly sat down on a nearby bench and watched as Noah pulled Aria under the boughs of the willow tree in the hotel gardens. Angel knew that place had a special significance to them. The tree was lit up with pumpkin fairy lights and under the boughs there was even a friendly-looking ghost, but Angel guessed that Aria wouldn't mind what creature was there to share their proposal.

Noah kissed Aria, wrapping his arms around her, and she smiled up at him. He swept a hair from her face.

'Aria...'

It seemed that Noah was having trouble finding the words. It seemed odd that a man that was used to negotiating the buying and selling of multi-million-pound hotels would struggle to find the words to secure this next partnership but Angel supposed that these words were probably the most important that Noah would ever say.

Aria stroked Noah's face and he let out a little laugh.

'I had a big speech planned for tonight, I've been practising it for days. But seeing you now under our willow tree, every word has gone out the window. Words don't seem to be enough to convey how utterly happy you make me, how my life has changed so much. There are no words in the world that could truly show you how much I love you. You are my everything, my entire world.'

Aria looked stunned and a bit confused. 'Wait, are you proposing to me? Is that what this is?'

'Well I'm trying if you'd let me finish.' Noah pulled back and got down on one knee. 'Aria—'

Aria suddenly launched herself at him, knocking him to the ground as she kissed him hard, squealing against his lips.

Angel laughed and Clover smiled, leaning her head against Angel's shoulder as they continued to watch.

'Aria, wait, I have a ring—'

'I don't care.' She kissed him again.

'Can I at least ask the question?'

'The answer is yes Noah. I love you completely and utterly. Yes I will marry you, of course I will.'

Noah smiled as she kissed him again.

'Well that's a resounding yes,' Angel said.

'God, they are the perfect poster couple for a happy ever after, aren't they,' Clover said.

They watched as Noah wrestled the ring box from his pocket and slid the ring on her finger, which made Aria squeal even more and kiss him again.

'Come on, let's go and offer our congratulations before this kiss gets even more heated,' Angel said.

'Good idea,' Clover said.

∼

Clover stroked Orion as she watched Angel light the fire. Watching her sister get engaged tonight, getting her happy ever after, Clover knew she wanted that too, that unconditional, unwavering love, finding her soul mate, spending forever with the man she loved. And she knew, in her heart, that man was Angel. The more time she spent with him, the more she was falling for him. But that didn't mean she was any closer to taking that step, and time was running out.

Angel sat back on the floor, his arms round his knees as he stared at the flames. The only noise in the room was the sound of the fire crackling.

She shifted Orion off her and went and sat next to him, stroking his back. He looked at her, smiling sadly.

'What are you thinking?' Clover said.

'I leave tomorrow.'

'I know.'

'And I'm going to miss you like crazy,' Angel said.

'I'm going to miss you too.'

That was an understatement. She was desperate to ask him to stay, they needed more time together to find out if they had any chance of a future but she wanted that to be his choice, she didn't want to feel like she was holding him back. And what could she offer him? She couldn't give him any promises for a future. She didn't know if she would ever be brave enough to take that chance with him. The scars Marcus had given her ran deep and she didn't know whether they would ever heal. If they'd had more time, a few months together, she might have found the courage to pursue a serious relationship, if that was what Angel wanted. But this was too soon. She wasn't ready and she had no idea if he even wanted that. He'd made it clear that she meant something to him, that this was more than just friends, but she had no idea how much more.

She stroked his face and he leaned into her hand.

'Yesterday, you said that things had changed between us, that it was more now. How much more?' Clover asked.

Angel turned to stare at the flames for a moment.

'It's more than I expected it to be,' he said quietly. 'And more than either of us wanted.'

He turned back to look at her.

She swallowed. 'People change.'

'Yes, that's true.' His eyes scanned her face.

They were both dancing around this when they didn't have the time to do that. He was leaving tomorrow.

'Angel, you've come to mean so much to me. This is way bigger than just two friends having sex.'

'For me too.'

'We have something special.'

He let out a heavy breath. 'This last week has been… incredible but…' He looked sad all of a sudden. 'But' did not sound good. He wasn't going to stay. This was goodbye for him.

She suddenly didn't want to hear it. She leaned forward and kissed him, stroking his face, and he kissed her back.

'Show me how much I mean to you,' she whispered.

He groaned against her mouth, shifting slightly so he could

lower her to the rug, where he continued to kiss her. He slowly started to undress her and she removed his clothes too. It wasn't hurried or desperate, it was careful, considered.

When they both were naked, he started kissing her all over, adoring every inch with his mouth and his hands as she stroked him, kissed him. He kissed up her thighs and then right there at the spot that was crying out with need for him. That feeling ripped through her so quickly, she arched up off the floor, desperate for him but unable to take any more. Her heart was thundering, her breath heavy as he moved over her and kissed her hard.

He fumbled around with a condom for a few moments and clarity slipped into her brain.

'Angel, I need you to know...'

He slid carefully inside her and all words went from her mouth, her mind clearing of everything but him, this moment now.

He stared down at her as if... he loved her. God her heart felt like it was going to burst, she was so full of him that it seemed as if she was brimming over. He kissed her and she felt her body melting around him as he started to move slowly against her.

He pulled back to look at her. 'When I look back on my life, this – you, us – will be the thing that means the most to me, the memory that will bring me the most joy. I could never ever look back at my life with regret because I had this time with you.'

Her heart roared in her chest, tears springing into her eyes. This man, she loved him so much, he was everything to her, but she couldn't bring herself to say those words. It would change everything between them and she simply wasn't ready for that.

He kissed her before she could say anything and she

wrapped her arms and legs around him, stroking his back, his hair, holding him tight as that was the only thing she could offer him right then.

He gathered her close, touching that spot, but it was her love for him that caused that feeling to build inside her again. He pulled back to gaze at her again and it was the look of complete adoration that caused her to fall over the edge. He kissed her hard and she moaned against his lips as he fell apart himself. He collapsed down on top of her and she held him tight, stroking down his back.

As she lay there, feeling his heart thunder against hers, she knew she'd never get over Angel. There was never going to be any coming back from this.

CHAPTER TWENTY-TWO

Clover watched as Angel gathered his stuff together, packing the last few bits into his rucksack and suitcase. He had been here only a week, but his stuff had migrated all over the cottage. She had always been a fairly tidy person but she was going to miss having his stuff here. The cottage was going to be empty without him.

They'd spent the morning in bed, making love, kissing, cuddling, touching as if they couldn't bear to be apart, but time had ticked on regardless of their desire to stay wrapped in each other's arms and eventually he'd had to get up and start packing.

She felt numb watching him get ready to leave. Those walls she'd built to protect herself, that Angel had so carefully pulled down over the last week, were slowly being rebuilt again.

She wanted to tell him how she felt, but the night before had definitely felt like goodbye from him. What would it achieve other than to make things awkward between them?

She looked away from the suitcase, wanting to focus on

anything else, and her eyes fell on the horse statue that her dad had given her mum as a symbol of his love for her. Her parents had seemingly had it so easy. He'd loved her, she'd loved him and that had been the only thing that mattered. Her dreams had become his dreams and they'd built a life together. There had never been any worry over whether they would be betrayed or hurt. They'd trusted each other completely.

'Well, I think that's everything,' Angel said, looking around, and Clover's heart plummeted into her stomach. 'Oh, my toothbrush, I always forget that.'

He ran back upstairs and for reasons she didn't fully understand she grabbed the horse statue and shoved it inside his rucksack, hidden underneath his hoodie, before zipping the rucksack back up.

He came back downstairs and unzipped his suitcase to put it inside his soap bag.

'Right, that really is everything this time.' He checked his watch. 'The taxi will be here any minute.'

She stood up. 'So I guess I'll see you in a few months.'

He nodded and silence fell over them as they stood staring at each other, a thousand words lying unspoken between them.

She opened her mouth to speak although she had no words at all.

A car beeped its horn outside.

'Well, that's me,' Angel said, then he paused. 'Take care of yourself, Clover. If you ever need anything, you know where I am.'

She nodded, willing her tears to stay at bay.

He stared at her. Clearly neither one of them wanted to say goodbye.

He bent to grab his suitcase and rucksack and then made his way over to the door.

'Wait, wait!' Clover said, hurrying over to him. She reached up and kissed him and he immediately dropped his bags, wrapping his arms around her and kissing her back. She couldn't help the tears falling.

He pulled back and his eyes clouded with concern. 'Hey, what are these tears for?' He wiped her cheeks gently. 'This isn't goodbye.'

'I know, I just...'

The car horn sounded again and Angel looked at his watch. 'I'm going to have to go. I have to get the ten o'clock train if I'm going to catch my flight.' He studied her face and then kissed her one last time.

He took a step back, picked up his bags and, with a last wistful look, he walked out the door.

She moved to the door and watched him get in the car, watched him wave as the car turned round in the tiny lane and drove away. She stood there waiting until the car disappeared through the trees.

She closed the door and leaned both hands against it as she burst into tears.

~

Clover walked into her office and was surprised to see Skye and Aria waiting for her. As soon as she saw their concerned faces, she found herself welling up again.

Aria immediately wrapped her arms around her as Skye quickly shut the office door and then joined in with the group hug.

Eventually they guided her to a chair and brought other chairs close to hers. They sat down.

'I take it he left?' Aria said.

'Yes, about an hour ago. He'll be on the train by now.'

'Did you tell him you loved him?' Skye said.

Clover shook her head. 'Wait, how did you know I loved him?'

Skye smiled sadly. 'Because I'm your sister.'

'But I didn't even know myself until yesterday...' she trailed off. Who was she kidding? She'd been in love with him for the last six months, she'd just been too scared to admit that, even to herself. 'Every time I tried to tell him, I just couldn't do it. Every time I thought about forever with Angel, I thought about the last time I wanted that and how spectacularly badly that went wrong. I was scared. I think we just needed more time for me to let my guard down, but now it's too late.'

'Why didn't you ask him to stay?' Aria said.

'Because I wanted him to make that choice, I didn't want to guilt him into staying. I think he'd always regret staying because of me. I wanted *him* to want that. And he didn't.' Tears welled in her eyes. 'Last night, when we were making love, I could see it was goodbye for him. And then when he left, he was... happy. He's excited about this new job. From the start, we both agreed this was something casual, that hadn't changed for him. And I can't even be angry with him. He has been so lovely to me throughout all of this. He was patient, kind and supportive.'

'I knew he was going to be trouble,' Skye teased, punching her hand menacingly. 'I should have roughed him up for being too bloody nice to you.'

Clover smiled, sadly. 'Persuaded him to be nasty to me instead?'

'Yes, something like that.'

'I don't think Angel has it in him.'

'No, sadly you picked one of the good ones there,' Skye said, begrudgingly.

Clover sighed and took the tissue that Aria passed her.

'This was never going to be a long-term thing. I knew that. I was happy with that until my stupid heart betrayed me.' She took a deep, bolstering breath. 'But I suppose this is a good thing. The whole point of this was to get me back into the dating saddle again. Now that Angel has fixed me and set the bar for what I'm looking for in a relationship, I can move on, date someone else.'

The thought of that brought fresh tears to her eyes. Marcus had ruined her for having relationships with other men and now Angel had done the same, although in a completely different way. He had set the bar so ridiculously high, no man was ever going to be able to compete with him.

Her sisters didn't seem convinced by this tactic either.

'It is possible that Angel didn't stay because he didn't know he had anything to stay for,' Aria said, carefully. 'If he believed that you still wanted something casual, then perhaps he thought there was no point in staying.'

Clover stared at her. That thought hadn't even occurred to her. She'd given him no sign that she wanted more, mainly because she was too scared to take that step. Would he have stayed if she'd told him she loved him?

'God, what am I going to do?'

'You could go after him,' Skye suggested.

Clover's eyes widened. 'Go to Rome?'

'Sure, you could do with a break.'

'He's going to that hotel with the view of buying it, he'll be having professional meetings with the manager and staff. Then I turn up like a deranged ex and beg him to come back. It's hardly a good look for him.'

'True,' Aria said. 'I just know that love doesn't come around very often and if you find someone you have those feelings for, then they are worth fighting for.'

'Aria, it took five years for you and Noah to get together.'

'It wasn't our time,' Aria said, awkwardly.

Clover sighed. 'Maybe it just wasn't our time too. Maybe, if we're supposed to be together, we'll get another chance at it when he comes home. And maybe I might have plucked up enough courage by then to take it.'

Angel sat on the plane, staring out of the window as it taxied onto the runway, with a horrible feeling in his gut that he had left something behind. But he knew it wasn't a toothbrush or a phone charger, it was something far more important than that.

He brushed his hair from his face. His stomach was churning, he felt tense.

Normally when he was going to a new place, he felt excited, and with this amazing job that Noah had offered him he should be looking forward to the challenge. He had always been sure of his path in his life – he wanted to travel, see every country, experience everything the world had to offer – but his life choices no longer seemed so clear. His future now felt empty, meaningless. The life he had chosen was not enough.

He took a sip of his water, his mouth feeling dry.

He could not forget the sight of Clover crying as he'd walked out the door. He'd played it over and over in his head a thousand times and it made him sick. How could he have left her when she was so upset? And why was she crying? He'd left Jewel Island several times over the last six months since they'd first met, and to his knowledge she had never cried before.

He felt awful. He'd promised he would be there for her as long as she needed him and he'd just walked away. Although maybe he shouldn't feel bad; if she'd asked him to stay, he would have done it in a heartbeat. How could he change the course of his life unless he knew that she wanted that, that she wanted him?

He remembered wiping her tears away and he rubbed his eyes, trying to dispel that image.

He wondered if her feelings had changed.

God, he should have told her how he felt. Even if she didn't feel the same way, she deserved to know. And how could he expect her to tell him how she felt if he couldn't do the same?

He had to forget this. This was only ever supposed to be something casual, they'd both agreed that. He was happy with his life as it was. He didn't need this complication. They'd both had fun and it had been wonderful but now was the time to draw a line under it.

He grabbed his bag, to retrieve the portfolio on the hotel he was about to go and see. He pulled his hoodie out and was surprised when he felt something heavy amongst the material. He felt around and found the wire horse he'd admired a few days before. The horse Clover's dad had gone to great lengths to get for her mum. Clover had called it a symbol of their love. And now she had given it to him.

He stared at the horse.

Christ, maybe she did love him after all.

He felt his carefully-mapped-out life crumbling away from him and it scared him.

She had no right to tell him like this. She should have said something before he left so they could have talked about this.

He shoved the horse back into his bag and threw the bag onto the floor.

He watched the plane take off, leaving England behind.

This was for the best.

CHAPTER TWENTY-THREE

Clover was attempting to have a bit of a lie-in, after spending several hours the night before prepping the restaurant for the Halloween ball that night. Aria, Noah, Skye, Jesse and several other members of staff had all helped to move tables around the edge of the room so there was a dance floor in the middle. Plus they had added loads of Halloween decorations and lights. It had been well past midnight when she had finally fallen into bed. She had slept badly as she hadn't been able to stop thinking about Angel, but her chances of a lie-in were getting further and further away.

She was half awake now and she could hear a distant banging. She couldn't work out where it was coming from, but it didn't seem to be stopping anytime soon.

She sat up and looked at her clock. It was seven o'clock. What could be making such a noise at this time in the morning?

She got out of bed and opened her bedroom door, the noise getting louder. She suddenly realised it was someone banging on her front door. Who the hell would be here at this time in the morning, knocking so hard as if the world had come to an end?

She ran downstairs and flung open the door and her heart leapt when she saw Angel standing on her doorstep. Christ, was she still dreaming? She wanted to throw herself into his arms, kiss him and drag him back to bed but this wasn't right. He should be in Rome by now.

'What are you doing here?'

She noticed he was holding the horse statue and he looked pissed.

'Why did you put this in my bag?'

Oh god. Why had she done that? She should have let him go, tried to move on. She wasn't ready for more so why flag up to him that her feelings had changed?

She cleared her throat. 'You came back to ask me that?'

She turned and went back inside, scooping up Orion as a much needed distraction.

Angel followed her in, still brandishing the horse. 'Why?'

'Because you said you liked it,' Clover shrugged, hoping to pull off an air of nonchalance. 'I can't believe you came back because I gave you a going-away gift. You could have just phoned to ask me. You had a bit of a wasted journey.'

'This felt too important to do over the phone. I think you gave me this because you love me.'

She stared at him. Of course he would think that. And in truth, she had wanted to tell him her feelings but hadn't been able to find the words. She'd been too scared of embracing that future with him. 'You're wrong.'

She hated how her voice caught when she said that and he clearly heard it.

'I don't think I am.'

Her heart was thundering against her chest. Her breath was heavy. She didn't want this.

'Would it help if I told you I love you?' Angel said.

She felt all her breath leave her in one big whoosh and she quickly sat down, holding Orion tighter until he wailed in protest and wiggled himself out of her arms, darting up the stairs. Now she had no protection.

'Did you hear what I said?'

'Yes, I heard, and no, it doesn't help.'

He stared at her. 'What?'

She pulled on a loose thread on her pyjamas, focussing her attention on watching it unravel, the stitching around her sleeve slowly coming undone. She had watched her dreams for a happy future unravel in the same way the day that Marcus had betrayed her. She swallowed a lump in her throat, the shame of falling for him, the humiliation of what he had done so fresh in her mind.

'The last time I heard those words they were from Marcus, as he was filming me having sex, with the intent of showing it to the whole world.'

Angel swore and knelt down in front of her, taking her hand.

'I would never do that to you. I can't promise that this is forever but, whatever happens between us, I can categorically promise it will never end like that.'

'I know.' Clover's voice wobbled and she shook her head. 'I can't do this. I didn't want this. I wanted something casual, fun.'

Angel stood up in frustration. 'Well so did I.'

'I didn't want forever.'

'Neither did I.'

'So what are you doing here?'

'I bloody love you,' Angel almost shouted. 'You've changed everything for me. Travelling the world, seeing the sights, none of it means anything anymore, not without you.'

Her throat was raw with suppressed emotion. This was everything she wanted to hear and everything she'd feared. She wanted to grab hold of this chance with him and push it away all at the same time.

'So now what? You've come back, you're going to stay, give up your life of travelling around the world for me? You will grow to resent me for it,' Clover said.

'I could never resent you.'

'You'd regret giving up your life for me.'

'If I was ever to look back at my life with regret, it would be because I never took this chance with you.'

She knew she would regret that too. She stared at the floor; this was too much too soon. She just wanted everything to go back to how it was, fun and silly, no strings.

'Look, I'm not saying I'm never going to travel again,' Angel said. 'This job is still something I'm interested in but I'm saying we can make this work, come up with a plan together. Maybe work with one hotel a year, where I'd be away for a few months, but spend most of the year here with you. You could come with me for a few weeks when I did go away, we can see the world together. I can fly back during quiet periods where I'm not needed. We can figure this out if you think we have something worth fighting for.'

She stared at him, tears brimming in her eyes again. She shook her head. 'I can't do this. I can't give you what you want.'

He stared at her. 'I'm not Marcus.'

'I know. You are the most wonderful man I have ever met. You are miles better than him in every single way. You are patient, kind, funny and my feelings for you far outweigh whatever I felt for him, but that means the potential to be hurt is far greater.'

He didn't say anything for the longest time. 'So you do love me?'

'You're not listening, I don't want this.'

'If we love each other, that's all that matters, we can figure out the rest.'

She stood up and moved to the kitchen, putting the kettle on for want of something to do.

Angel followed her in. 'Do you love me?'

She turned round to face him and she willed herself to tell him how she felt, to take a step forward and kiss him and tell him she did want that future with him. But she just couldn't do it.

'You shouldn't have come.'

He took a step back and then another, his face filled with hurt.

'You're right, we agreed it was something casual.' His voice was broken.

She watched as he carefully replaced the horse back on the mantelpiece and then moved towards the door.

She felt sick.

He turned back to face her.

'I'm in the Sapphire Suite tonight and I'll be taking the first flight back to Rome early tomorrow and this time I won't be coming back… Unless you give me something to stay for.'

She had no words at all to stop him.

He turned and walked out the door.

She sat down on the sofa, her head in her hands.

All she'd wanted was a normal relationship with a wonderful man and that was what Angel was offering her. So why the hell couldn't she take it?

~

Angel sat in his suite, staring out at the views over Sapphire Bay.

God, what a mess.

Clover was his future; he was sure of that. The rest of it, his job, where they were in the world, they could work out along the way. But she had built those walls around her heart many years ago and he had no idea how to reach her.

There was a knocking on the door and his heart leapt. Had she changed her mind already?

He quickly ran to answer it and felt his heart sink when he saw Noah standing on the other side.

He opened the door wider for his boss to come in. He was surely going to be pissed. Noah had set up the meetings with the owner and manager of the hotel in Rome and now all of that would have to be postponed or cancelled.

'Aria just told me you were here, what happened?' Noah said.

'I'm sorry, mate. I just...' he shook his head. 'I couldn't do it. I did contact the hotel and tell them that something had come up and we would have to reschedule. I'm sorry to let you down.'

'I don't care about that. There will always be other hotels to buy, if that's what you want. All I care about is that you're OK.'

Angel sat down in the chair near the window and Noah sat opposite him.

'It's Clover.'

'I thought it might be.'

'I love her.'

'Yeah, I guessed as much. I'm sorry, I should never have complicated things with this job when I knew you were starting something with her. I had a feeling it would turn serious between you. You two have always had an amazing connection. I'm sorry I ruined things with my offer.'

'Don't be sorry for that. It's an amazing opportunity. You weren't to know it would turn out like this, hell I had no idea it would turn out like this either.'

'So you came back and told her you loved her?' Noah asked.

Angel nodded, brushing his hand through his hair.

'And I'm guessing from the fact that you're here and not celebrating your reunion with her that it didn't go well?'

'You could say that. She's scared.'

'And I don't blame her,' Noah said.

'I know. What happened to her was horrible, but she must know I'm never going to do that to her.'

'I think she knows that, but I'm guessing things are moving too fast for her. She needs time to get her head round the idea of a serious relationship, of something more long-term. You've been back a week and everything has changed for her.'

'This was always going to be serious between us, we were both kidding ourselves if we thought otherwise.'

'That may be the case but she's not ready to admit that to herself yet.'

Angel groaned. 'Am I being a complete asshole?'

'God, no, you love her. And I'm pretty sure she's in love with you too. Aria told me about her ex. It's just a complicated mess because of what he did to her. This isn't your fault.'

Angel sighed. 'So what do I do?'

Noah looked out over the view for a moment. 'I'm not an expert in love. I had one serious relationship before Aria and that was a complete disaster. When I came here I was too scared to get involved with Aria in case I messed everything up. But she was a persistent little thing,' he smirked.

'So be persistent?'

'No, well kind of. Look, the way I see it you have two options. You go to Rome and Australia for the next four to six weeks, and hope that during that time absence makes the heart grow fonder and Clover decides she wants more by the time you come back.'

Angel didn't like the sound of that. Clover could quite as easily forget him or move on with someone else now that he had apparently fixed her.

'Or you take her to the ball tonight and tell her nothing has to change, that you're here for as long as it takes for her to trust you, to be ready to have a proper relationship. Be patient with her.'

He could do that.

'But what about Rome?' Angel said.

'It can wait. And if you decide you want to stay here for the rest of your life, that's totally fine too. Falling in love with Aria has changed my life, so believe me I can understand if you change your mind and don't want to go.'

Angel sat back in his chair. He could be patient; he could take his time with this. He just hoped that Clover would agree to those terms and not push him away now she knew his feelings had changed.

Clover sat on the edge of the plunge pool at the bottom of the waterfall, her bare feet dipping into the cool water, her mind a swirl of confusion, just like the pool, churning with the force of the water that was tumbling into it.

'Isn't that cold?'

Clover looked up to see Sylvia O'Hare, in her trusted purple cloak. She looked particularly dramatic as the cloak flew around her.

'Hello Sylvia.' Clover managed a small smile. 'It's not too bad, you get used to it after a few minutes.'

Sylvia nodded and then, to Clover's surprise, she came over, took off her boots and bright red, stripy socks and sat down next to her, dipping her feet into the water too.

'Oh lord, that is cold,' Sylvia said, although she didn't remove her feet.

Clover smiled. She was such a spirited old lady, she had travelled the world, seen it all and was currently on her sixth husband.

'Sylvia, can I ask you something?'

'Sure.'

'You've been married a lot of times in your life.'

'Clive is number six,' Sylvia said. 'And hopefully my last.'

'And if you don't mind me asking, what were the reasons the other marriages came to an end?'

Sylvia started counting on her fingers. 'Michael was a big gambler, stole all my money to pay off his debts. Joseph tried to kill me, Alexander cheated on me with his secretary, which was rather boring and predictable. Jimmy cheated on me with everything that moved. William turned out to be gay, took him seventy years to figure it out, but he's married to a nice young man called Thomas now so he's happy. We keep in touch.'

Clover smiled. Sylvia was so blasé about it all, even about her second husband who had thrown her overboard from his yacht after an argument, a story she'd heard before.

'You've been let down so badly with the men you loved. How did you trust your next husband enough to marry him, knowing he could betray you too?'

'Oh honey, there was no way I was going to let any of these men have any impact on my future happiness. I cried over them of course, but then I dusted myself off and carried on.

There is a risk you could get hurt again, of course there is, but life is a risk. You could be out one day and get hit by a car, you could go skiing and break a leg or get buried in an avalanche, you could go for a swim and drown, or you could stay in your house every day where it's safe and die of a heart attack. Life is to be lived, not to be spent hiding away. The way I have always lived my life is to do something that scares me, take a tiny risk every day. Sometimes that's eating a strange food or buying a ridiculous cloak my ex-husband said I'd never wear.' Sylvia picked up her flamboyant cloak and let it drop. 'Or sticking my feet in a freezing cold waterfall. Life is much more enjoyable when you push on the walls of that little safe bubble.'

Clover smiled. 'Angel said something similar.'

'He's a good man,' Sylvia said.

'He is, he's wonderful,' Clover said.

'But you were hurt in the past and you want to know if you can trust him not to hurt you?'

'Insightful, but yes.'

'Someone once said, "The best way to know if you can trust someone is to trust them." People can only prove they are trustworthy if you give them the chance. Trust is not going to happen overnight, it takes time. But if you love him then it's definitely worth the risk.'

Clover nodded. If anyone was worth the risk it was Angel. There was no point in trying to protect herself from getting hurt, when pushing him away and not being with him was hurting anyway.

CHAPTER TWENTY-FOUR

Clover wiped her hands down her dress, took a deep breath and knocked on the door of Angel's suite.

A few moments later, Angel answered. He studied her face and then stepped back to let her in.

'I'm glad you're here,' he said. 'I've been going over what I wanted to say to you for hours and—'

'Listen, before you say anything, I have something I want to say first.'

He stared at her and then nodded, but now he was there directly in front of her, she was having trouble finding the right words, when actually there were only three little words she needed to say. She knew what Sylvia has said was true, she had to push the boundaries, do something that scared her, and handing over her heart was the scariest thing she could do.

'I love you,' Clover blurted out, before she could talk her way out of it. She heard the words from her mouth and surprisingly they didn't sound as terrifying as she thought they would. She tried again. 'I love you.'

Angel stared at her and a huge smile appeared on his face.

In two large strides he was in front of her, cupping her face and kissing her hard. She wrapped her arms around his neck, kissing him back. She couldn't help the tears of relief falling down her cheeks.

He pulled back slightly to look at her. 'I love you too, I think I always have. You were the one woman I could never forget.'

He bent his head again to kiss her but she put a hand on his chest to stop him.

He frowned in confusion.

'I told you before that I'm broken and being in love with you doesn't change that. I want this with you, I want a future with you, but I'm still scared.'

He nodded. 'I was an ass for pushing you, nothing has to change between us. I'm not going to be talking about marriage and babies any time soon. We can just carry on exactly as we were before without any deadlines. I will show you every single day that I love you, that I can be trusted, that I would never hurt you. And when you're ready, be that six months or six years from now, we can talk about the future then. I'm not going anywhere.'

She frowned. 'What about your trip to Rome, your new job? I don't want to stop you following your dreams.'

'It can wait. Things are so new between us and nothing is more important to me right now than you. Maybe next spring I can look for a hotel to work with then, but now I just want to focus on us.'

She smiled. 'I like the sound of that.'

She leaned up to kiss him, pressing herself against him. He bent and lifted her, carrying her over to the bed as the kiss continued. They undressed each other very quickly as they touched and kissed each other. He grabbed a condom and a few moments later he was inside her. He moved to kiss her but she stopped him again.

'I have one more question.'

'What's that?'

'Do you have a costume for tonight's ball?'

He laughed. 'I have the perfect thing.'

Clover couldn't stop giggling as Angel held her in his arms as they moved around the dance floor.

She'd gone for a typical witch costume and, although the black dress she'd bought online was a little bit more figure-hugging than she would have liked, Angel definitely seemed to approve. She'd teamed it with stripy green and black knee-high socks and had put green streaks in her hair.

Angel was wearing his blue ballet tights, teamed with tight red shorts over the top and his Superman t-shirt. He'd even managed to tie his red t-shirt around his neck so it hung behind him like a cloak. He looked ridiculous and Noah had already shown his disapproval.

Sylvia, who was sweeping around the room in a dramatic black and red cloak, had already given her the thumbs up of approval after admiring Angel's bum for a few minutes.

Clover rested her head on his chest as they moved and watched the hotel guests and villagers dancing around the room too. Everyone seemed to be having a good time. She smiled when she saw Jesse dancing around the room with Skye hanging off him, her feet off the ground as he held her against him, his strong arms wrapped around her back to keep her up. She noticed Aria dancing with Noah, staring up at him with a big smile on her face. Noah bent his head and gave her a sweet kiss.

'What are you thinking?' Angel said and Clover turned her head to face him. He stroked her cheek. 'You have a big smile on your beautiful face.'

'Lots of things. I'm thinking how happy my sisters look, I'm thinking that the ball seems to have been a big success. Mostly I'm thinking how ridiculous you look in this silly costume and how much I love you for wearing it. Well, how much I love you for everything really. I never thought for one second I would fall in love again but you made that part very easy, even if I didn't want to admit it.'

He smiled. 'You have made my life complete. I was always searching for the next thing, I didn't want to miss out on anything, I didn't want to look back on my life with regret, but you would have been the one thing I would have regretted missing out on. My life felt empty before and now it feels full. I love you and I cannot wait to start the rest of my life with you.'

She smiled and leaned up to kiss him.

'Excuse me, can I cut in?'

Clover turned to look at Jesse in confusion, who was standing there waiting to dance with her.

She glanced at Angel who was looking as confused as she was.

'Oh sure,' Clover said. Stepping out of Angel's arms, she opened her arms to dance with Jesse instead but, to her surprise, Jesse swept Angel into his arms and started dancing with him.

Clover laughed as Angel just went along with it, snuggling his head against Jesse's ample chest.

She turned around, knowing her sisters would have something to do with this, and sure enough Skye and Aria were waiting for her. She moved over to them and hugged them both.

'Are you OK?' Skye asked. 'Although your huge smile says it all.'

'I'm blissfully, perfectly, utterly overjoyed.'

Skye grinned.

'I'm so happy for you,' Aria said. 'He is perfect for you. Is he staying then?'

'For a few months at least, he says he's not in any hurry to leave me right now. Maybe in the spring he might go away for a few months and maybe I might go with him. I'm sure we can work it out. For now, we are just going to take some time to get to know each other properly.'

She turned to face the dance floor again, her arms looped around both of her sisters.

'They make a cute couple, don't they,' Clover said, watching Angel and Jesse.

'The man's an idiot,' Skye said, fondly, watching her ex-husband. 'But I love him.'

'Then maybe you need to tell him that,' Clover said.

Skye nodded. 'One day I will.'

The song came to an end and Angel and Jesse let go of each other. Angel came back over to Clover and took her back into his arms, moving back onto the dance floor.

'You're a much nicer dance partner than Jesse,' Angel whispered in her ear.

She laughed. 'I think if we're going to be permanent dance partners, you might need to learn how to dance properly.'

He grinned. 'I'm up for the challenge.'

EPILOGUE

CHRISTMAS DAY

Clover looked around the lounge of her cottage and smiled with love for her family. The log fire was crackling and dancing in the fireplace, the fairy lights around the tree were twinkling. It looked cosy and happy. It had been a wonderful Christmas Day with Angel, her sisters and their other halves. They had played games, watched Christmas movies, made snowmen in the snow that had unexpectedly appeared the day before and eaten way too much. Although Aria and Noah had been up at the hotel overseeing the Christmas dinner and meetings with Santa, they had spent most of their time here with them. Clover looked over at them now, Aria sitting on Noah's lap as they talked quietly to each other. She glanced over at Skye, who had Jesse's daughter Bea, cuddled up on her lap as they both drank the Christmas-cake-flavoured hot chocolate Jesse had made for everyone. Jesse was on the floor, one arm over Skye's legs, as he played with Orion.

Clover looked at Angel, sitting next to her on the sofa, and he kissed the top of her head. Her life had changed so much over the last few months. Every day with him had made those fears she had lived with for three years slowly ebb away. She knew she loved him now so much more than she had before. She knew this was forever and she had already caught herself many times thinking about a future with him.

Snow was falling thick and fast outside, as it had been for most of the day, and Angel had already talked about going out for a late-night walk in the snow once everyone had left. There wasn't much left of the day now.

The day before, the hotel had held their first wedding – a small affair, but Jacob and Ruby Harrington had looked blissfully in love. Because of the snow, the Christmassy wedding photos had looked particularly magical and Clover knew Angel had taken some brilliant shots for the website.

Their own fake wedding shoot in the autumn had generated quite a bit of interest from couples planning to hold their wedding and the hotel already had seventeen weddings booked for the following year.

Bea yawned sleepily.

Jesse stood up. 'I think we better get home to bed.'

Bea stood up and stretched and her father put an arm around her to steady her. She was getting so tall now, she'd soon be overtaking Skye, but as Jesse was so big, it was clear his daughter was taking after him.

'Before you go, we have a bit of announcement,' Aria said. She looked at Noah with a smile. 'The adoption agency has found a match for us. A little girl called Orla, she's five years old and we're going to meet her on the twenty-seventh. We had the phone call yesterday to confirm. If all goes well, she'll be coming to live with us early January.'

'Oh my god, that's so exciting,' Clover said, hugging her.

'You're going to be parents,' Skye said, leaping up to hug Aria and Noah.

Angel clapped Noah on the back before giving him a hug. 'That's brilliant news, I'm so happy for you, mate.'

'That's wonderful news,' Jesse said. 'Having a daughter will change your life.'

Bea laughed in mock outrage. 'For good or for bad?'

Jesse kissed his daughter's forehead. 'Good, definitely.'

They all bundled themselves up in their coats, hats and scarves and, after a few hugs, everyone left.

'Shall we go out for a walk?' Angel said. 'I'd love to get some photos of the gardens and the hotel in the snow.'

'Sounds good,' Clover said, wrapping herself in her coat and hat, before they stepped outside.

Angel started taking pictures. Clover looked up at the inky night sky as snowflakes swirled and danced around them. The gardens were completely silent, the only sound the snow crunching under their feet, no one else around. The fairy lights were twinkling and sparkling under the snow, the trees branches heavy with it. The whole place looked magical, it couldn't be more perfect. And to put the cherry on the cake she was holding hands with the man she loved. The year before she had stood on top of the headland, looking out over the island and wishing she could finally move on from what happened in her past, that she could stop being scared. She had well and truly ticked that box.

She glanced up at him as he took another photo. She smiled.

He caught her looking and bent his head to kiss her. 'God, I love you Clover Philips.'

She smiled against his lips. 'I love you too.'

He wrapped his arms around her, holding her close against him as the snow fell around them.

'Now listen, I have a little dilemma you might be able to help me with. I've spoken to Noah and Jesse about this and

I've even spoken to your sisters but I think maybe I should talk to you.'

'OK,' Clover said, in confusion. What would he have talked about with her sisters that he hadn't talked about with her?

'As my best friend, what would be your advice in this situation? You see, there's this woman I've been dating for the last few months.' Angel stroked her cheek, his eyes filled with adoration for her. 'And she is incredible. She's smart, brave, brilliant, funny and I have fallen head over heels in love with her.'

Clover smiled. 'She sounds nice.'

'Oh she is.'

'So what's the dilemma?'

'Well, when we first started seeing each other she wasn't looking for anything serious, we agreed we wouldn't really talk about a future. But as time has gone on, I want that future with her – marriage, children, forever – more than anything. I had thought about proposing to her but I don't know if she's ready for that and I didn't want to do anything to scare her off. Things between us have never been better and I don't want to do anything to ruin that.'

Clover's heart roared in her chest as she stared at him. He wanted to propose. But there was not one single ounce of fear in her mind. It had come along a lot sooner than she'd expected but she wanted that future too. It felt right.

'What do you think?' Angel said. 'Should I propose, or should I wait?'

She swallowed down the huge lump of emotion in her throat. 'I think she's a very lucky woman having someone like you love her, someone who is patient and kind. Someone who puts her needs and wants above your own. I think if you were to ask her to marry you, she'd definitely say yes.'

He stared at her, his eyes scanning her face, and then he

broke into a huge smile. 'I didn't want to spoil the surprise but I thought maybe I should tell her before, so she had time to think about it before I launched it on her.'

'I think that's a very good idea.'

He smiled and kissed her and then took her hand and carried on walking as if nothing had just happened.

'Wait, are we not going to talk about how you're going to do it?'

He laughed. 'You won't have to wait long. I have a plan.'

She smiled and leaned her head against him, wondering if he was going to do it on New Year's Eve or whether he'd do it sooner than that. She'd never felt so completely happy and content in her life before.

They came to a fork in the path and, instead of taking the path back to her cottage, they took the path that would lead them over the headland towards the village. Maybe Angel wanted to take some photos of the village. She didn't mind, the whole winter wonderland was incredibly romantic.

She reached her favourite spot of the headland, underneath her treehouse, the rest of the island spread out beneath them, the houses twinkling in the darkness, the roofs covered in a thick blanket of snow.

Angel paused, taking another photo with his phone.

'It's beautiful, isn't it,' Clover said.

He turned and took a photo of her and she laughed. 'Not as beautiful as you.'

'Oh stop,' she waved it away.

'I've made you a video,' Angel said, swiping a few things on his phone, 'I have spent my life taking pictures of the places and experiences that mean the most to me and I wanted you to see the most important and significant ones.'

He swiped a few times across the screen and then handed

her the phone and she saw a video that was titled 'The best moments of my life'.

She pressed play and straightaway a photo of her came up on the screen. At the bottom was a caption that said, 'The day we met'.

She remembered that day; their connection had been instant, like two friends who had known each other their entire lives. They'd laughed and chatted and, while he'd been showing her his photos on his camera, he'd taken this snap of her.

The next photo was of them together at the festival of light in the spring, captioned, 'The first time I asked you out'. Angel was smiling in the photo, his arm around her as they took a selfie. She'd turned him down and he hadn't seemed to care. It hadn't changed their friendship at all. He'd told her then that he thought she was worth waiting for.

There were several more photos of her then that had been taken over the last eight months, her on the beach, the two of them together. Her dressed as a pumpkin. Them lying in bed together. She swallowed the lump of emotion in her throat as she realised the best moments of Angel's life were with her. As the video continued, she saw the photo he'd taken in this exact spot a few months before when they had been going on their date to the restaurant. It was captioned, 'The night I realised I was in love with you'.

Her eyes snapped to his and he was smiling. 'Keep watching.'

She returned her gaze to the screen, her eyes filling.

There were a few more photos of her and them together and then she saw the photo he'd taken just a few moments before and it was captioned, 'The night you said yes'.

She gasped and looked up at him. He was holding out a ring box.

'Clover Philips, you have filled my life with something I never knew I needed. In the short time we've known each other, you have given me the best memories of my life. Tonight is the start of making new memories together. I love you so much.' Angel dropped to one knee and opened the box. 'Will you marry me?'

She nodded, not even looking at the ring; she couldn't take her eyes off him. 'Of course I will. You are everything to me. I can't wait to start the rest of my life with you. I love you, completely and utterly.'

He smiled and stood up, sliding the ring on her finger, and she glanced at it for the first time. It was a gold, champagne-coloured stone that sparkled in the light.

'It's a topaz. The colour reminded me of you, how you brought light to my life.'

She smiled and leaned up and kissed him.

She giggled. 'When you said you wanted to propose, I thought you meant you'd do it in a few days.'

'I said you wouldn't have to wait long. I wanted to surprise you a little.'

She laughed. 'It was the best kind of surprise. That video was wonderful.'

'You mean the world to me and I wanted you to know that.' Angel stroked her cheek.

'Why don't you take me home and I'll show you how much you mean to me.'

He grinned. 'I'd like that very much.'

⁓

If you enjoyed *Autumn Skies over Ruby Falls*, you'll love my next gorgeously romantic story, *Ice Creams at Emerald Cove* out in March.

STAY IN TOUCH...

To keep up to date with the latest news on my releases, just go to the link below to sign up for a newsletter. You'll also get two FREE short stories, get sneak peeks, booky news and be able to take part in exclusive giveaways. Your email will never be shared with anyone else and you can unsubscribe at any time
https://www.subscribepage.com/hollymartinsignup

Website: https://hollymartin-author.com/
Email: holly@hollymartin-author.com
Twitter: @HollyMAuthor

Christmas at Mistletoe Cove

Juniper Island Series

Christmas Under a Cranberry Sky

A Town Called Christmas

White Cliff Bay Series

Christmas at Lilac Cottage

Snowflakes on Silver Cove

Summer at Rose Island

Standalone Stories

Fairytale Beginnings

Tied Up With Love

A Home on Bramble Hill

One Hundred Christmas Proposals

One Hundred Proposals

The Guestbook at Willow Cottage

For Young Adults

The Sentinel Series

The Sentinel (Book 1 of the Sentinel Series)

The Prophecies (Book 2 of the Sentinel Series)

The Revenge (Book 3 of the Sentinel Series)

The Reckoning (Book 4 of the Sentinel Series)

A LETTER FROM HOLLY

Thank you so much for reading *Autumn Skies over Ruby Falls*, I had so much fun creating this story and revisiting the beautiful Jewel Island. I hope you enjoyed reading it as much as I enjoyed writing it.

One of the best parts of writing comes from seeing the reaction from readers. Did it make you smile or laugh, did it make you cry, hopefully happy tears? Did you fall in love with Angel and Clover as much as I did? Did you like the gorgeous little Jewel Island? If you enjoyed the story, I would absolutely love it if you could leave a short review on Amazon. Getting feedback from readers is amazing and it also helps to persuade other readers to pick up one of my books for the first time.

My next book, out in March, is called *Ice Creams at Emerald Cove*. It's the third book in the Jewel Island Series and follows Skye and Jesse's story.

Thank you for reading.

Love Holly x

ACKNOWLEDGEMENTS

To my family, my mom, my biggest fan, who reads every word I've written a hundred times over and loves it every single time, my dad, my brother Lee and my sister-in-law Julie, for your support, love, encouragement and endless excitement for my stories.

For my twinnie, the gorgeous Aven Ellis for just being my wonderful friend, for your endless support, for cheering me on, for reading my stories and telling me what works and what doesn't and for keeping me entertained with wonderful stories. I love you dearly.

To my lovely friends Julie, Natalie, Jac, Verity and Jodie, thanks for all the support.

To the Devon contingent, Paw and Order, Belinda, Lisa, Phil, Bodie, Kodi and Skipper. Thanks for keeping me entertained and always being there.

To everyone at Bookcamp, you gorgeous, fabulous bunch, thank you for your wonderful support on this venture.

Thanks to the brilliant Emma Rogers for the gorgeous cover design.

Thanks to my fabulous editors, Celine Kelly and Rhian McKay.

To all the wonderful bloggers for your tweets, retweets, facebook posts, tireless promotions, support, encouragement and endless enthusiasm. You guys are amazing and I couldn't do this journey without you.

To anyone who has read my book and taken the time to tell me you've enjoyed it or wrote a review, thank you so much.

Thank you, I love you all.

Paperback ISBN 978-1-913616-17-5
Large Print ISBN 978-1-913616-18-2

Cover design by Emma Rogers

Printed in Great Britain
by Amazon

47142355R00151